Lost & Found Friend

GINNY WILLIAMS

HARVEST HOUSE PUBLISHERS
Eugene, Oregon 97402

LOST-AND-FOUND FRIEND

Copyright © 1994 by Ginny Williams
Published by Harvest House Publishers
Eugene, Oregon 97402

Library of Congress Cataloging-in-Publication Data

Williams, Ginny, 1957-
        Lost-and-found-friend / Ginny Williams.
            p.   cm. — (Class of 2000 ; bk. 3)
        Summary: Kelly, Julie, and Greg pray for their friend Brent
who is losing interest in life following his parents' divorce.
        ISBN 1-56507-220-0
        [1. Friendship—Fiction.   2. Divorce—Fiction.
3. Suicide—Fiction.   4. Christian life—Fiction.]
I. Title.   II. Series: Williams, Ginny, 1957–
Class of 2000 ; bk. 3.
PZ7.W65919Lo   1994
[Fic]—dc20   93-43949
                                                                CIP
                                                                AC

Printed in the United States of America.

94 95 96 97 98 99 00 01 — 10 9 8 7 6 5 4 3 2 1

To Mom

*Thanks for always being there
and for always believing*

ONE

As usual, French grammar and verb usage weren't consuming all of Kelly's attention. For the last fifteen minutes she had been checking her watch every thirty seconds or so. Thanksgiving Break had been too wonderful, so she was having a hard time bringing her brain back to school. What made it worse was that this was the *end* of the week. Five days should have helped her refocus on studying. But there were just too many other things to think about.

Finally, the bell rang. Grabbing her books, Kelly linked arms with her best friend, sixteen-year-old Julie Parker, and dragged her toward the door.

"Hey, what's the big rush? You act like you're on your way to a fire or something."

"I'm just ready for this week to be over," Kelly said.

"Yeah? Well, running to lunch isn't going to make it go any faster, you know."

Kelly didn't respond. Her pace didn't slacken either. She gave absentminded smiles to friends as she maneuvered through the crowds in the hallways of Kingsport High. Her bright blue eyes flashed excitement, and her long coppery curls bounced atop her slender shoulders.

Julie continued to protest against the pace they were setting. "They're not going to run out of food before we get there. And where's Greg? He always meets you outside of French and walks with us. Why aren't we waiting for him?"

Kelly smiled and continued to plow ahead, tossing her reply over her shoulder. "He's helping his chemistry teacher set up some big experiment. He said he would join us at our table. But he'll have to look for us. I want to get a table by the window."

Julie gave her a questioning look. "I want to watch the snow when it starts falling," Kelly explained.

Julie stopped abruptly just as they reached the cafeteria and stared at her friend. "You mean, I've been running down the halls like a fool because you want to watch it *snow*? Are you nuts? What makes you think it's going to snow?"

Kelly grabbed a tray and handed one to Julie. "It just has to snow! Wouldn't it be the perfect way to get the Christmas season off to a great start? I listened to the weather this morning. The weatherman said we had a good chance of flurries today. I always like to watch the first snow." Reaching down, she grabbed the baked chicken, rice, and vegetables staring up enticingly at her. "Hmm. Not bad for a Friday." Shoving a roll into her mouth, Kelly headed toward an empty table next to the window.

Julie followed closely and set her tray down next to Kelly's. She laughed as her friend pressed her face to the glass. "I don't see any huge snowflakes yet," she teased.

"You just wait. They're coming. You just have to have faith." She turned back to the table. "Where's Brent?" she asked. "Isn't he joining us today?"

"I'm right here." A male voice sounded just above her shoulder. "My soccer coach was giving me some information about the upcoming soccer tournament. That's why I'm late." Brent Jackson's voice was as open and friendly as his face. His curly brown hair, still damp from his shower after gym, combined with his dancing brown eyes almost gave him the look of a little boy. The strong athletic body that made him a star player on the soccer team spoke of his manhood. He was sixteen and also a junior. Setting down his loaded tray, he grabbed a chair and eased his body into it.

Brent was the perfect fit for Julie's blonde cuteness. Her bubbly personality and warmth made her a favorite at Kingsport High. The two had been dating since September. In that time the four of them—Kelly, Greg, Julie, and Brent—had become inseparable. Everything seemed more fun when they did it together.

"Trying to hide from me, are you? Never fear, woman! I will always find you."

Kelly shrieked when Greg pressed an ice cube up against her neck. "Hey! Watch it! What are you doing?"

"If you weren't so busy staring out the window, you might be aware of what's going on around you," Greg laughed. "Why did you switch tables? What's happening out there, anyway?" Adding his tray to the collection on the table, he leaned over to peer out.

"Nothing. Absolutely nothing." Kelly's voice was morose.

"You're staring at nothing?"

Kelly had to smile at the tone of Greg's voice. She supposed she did look a little funny with her face pressed to the glass. She sat back and gazed at her handsome boyfriend. His tall, toned body looked good in the jeans and blue sweater he was wearing. The color brought out the vividness of his eyes that were so like Kelly's. She also loved his short, wavy, black hair, but it was his smile that still made her heart turn. She and Greg had been special friends since April. Just in the last few months had she become confident enough to label them as boyfriend and girlfriend. It didn't really matter, though. Labels or not, he was simply her best friend.

"She's waiting for the snow." Julie's words were bland.

Greg cast a speculative look at Kelly and then smiled. "I had a feeling you were a 'first snow of the year' person."

"Thank you so much for not making fun of me." Kelly flashed him a brilliant smile. "I just *love* snow! I'd never want to live up north where it snows all the time, but December is designed for snow. Do you know we haven't had a white Christmas in twenty-five years around here? The weatherman said we're going to have a cold winter and that we'll have a good chance this year. Wouldn't that be great?"

"It sure would," Greg agreed enthusiastically. "We didn't have white Christmases where I lived in

Texas. I don't know that watching the sky will make it come, but I'll be just as happy as you if it does!"

He understands, Kelly thought to herself as she turned from the window and focused her attention on her three friends. They had a lot to talk about before the weekend.

"My dad called last night, Greg," Brent said as the foursome began to polish off their food. "He's got reservations for us at some posh hotel in D.C. for next weekend. It's about a four-hour trip, so he's going to pick us up here as soon as classes get out."

Greg nodded. "I'm really looking forward to going. I've always wanted to see Washington, D.C., but it was kind of a long drive from Texas. It's great of your dad to want me to go along."

"He said I could bring anyone I wanted, and my first choice was you. D.C. is neat. There are a lot of things I want to show you while we're there." Brent's contagious smile became teasingly smug as he turned to Kelly and Julie. "Do you think you two can survive without us for a weekend?"

Kelly's retort was quick. "Survive? We're looking forward to your leaving. Julie and I need some girl time. The last time we took y'all shopping at the mall, you couldn't behave, and we need to get our Christmas shopping done. Besides that, we're working on something..." She allowed her voice to trail off mysteriously as Julie nodded her head vigorously in agreement.

Greg looked indignant. "What do you mean we didn't behave ourselves? Just because Brent didn't look too good in that blue dress he tried on..."

"Yeah, it's not my fault it didn't fit right. I thought Greg looked pretty good in his flowered housecoat, though, didn't you?"

The girls groaned as they laughed helplessly and relived their embarrassment from a few weeks ago when the guys had joined them in the sportswear section of the local department store. Kelly and Julie had both wanted to melt into the floor when Greg and Brent walked up in women's clothing and put their arms around them. It was an unforgettable moment.

Kelly finally managed to bring herself back under control and fixed the boys with a stern stare. "Now you know exactly why we'll be glad to have you out of town next weekend. I don't want to have to explain you two to any more of Dad and Peggy's friends! It's like the whole town knows!"

As their laughter died down, the talk turned to different subjects.

"Will you guys be home in time for the youth group Christmas party?" Julie asked. "I know you've said before you will be, but does your dad know what time you have to be back?"

"We'll be back on time," Brent reassured her quickly. "I wouldn't miss the party for anything. Did you hear that we're going to have a hayride? I don't know how Martin is going to pull this one off. We're supposed to be meeting at the church, and I know we can't do a hayride through the city. We wanted to last year but decided it wouldn't be safe. It'll be interesting to see what he comes up with."

"The next few weeks are going to be really busy," Greg commented.

"You got that right," Kelly agreed. "I think that's why I've had such a hard time getting back into studying. There is so much fun stuff happening that it doesn't seem fair to have to study in the midst of it. I think they should just call off school for the whole month of December!" Kelly made a face to emphasize her words.

Her three friends merely laughed at her.

"You just want to sit around and watch for snow all month."

Julie's comment caused Kelly to turn and gaze out the window again, but her hopes were dashed once more. The sky was gray, but it was definitely dry.

"Anyway," Julie continued, "I found out this morning that our big Christmas concert is definitely the Wednesday of our last week of school. Mrs. Marrs, my music teacher, was afraid she was going to have to change it, but it's set in concrete now. I'll have rehearsal every Monday through Thursday afternoon until then. Y'all are coming, aren't you?"

Nodding heads made her smile in satisfaction.

"And you're all coming to the big indoor soccer tournament the Saturday before Christmas, right?" Brent asked. "We're having ten schools in. It should be a lot of fun, and I think we stand a pretty good chance of winning this year."

"We'll be there to cheer you on," Greg said. "We wouldn't miss a chance to watch the star player of the soccer team in action."

"I'll try not to disappoint you," Brent smiled.

Kelly looked at her watch. "Yikes!" she exclaimed. "We only have five minutes before class. Is everyone still okay for this afternoon and tonight?"

They all nodded enthusiastically. Kelly's step-mother, Peggy, was picking them all up after school, and they were headed out to the barn for an afternoon of riding. Then they were going back to Kelly's house for dinner, a movie, and games.

"How are things going with you and Peggy?"

Kelly flashed a smile at Julie. "It couldn't be going better. I can't believe how afraid I was to let her get close to me. I'm so glad God broke down my walls." Kelly's heart warmed as she thought of her stepmother. She would never forget her real mother who had died of cancer, but she was glad to have a mom again after having just her dad and her sister, Emily, for five years. She and her dad had been really close, but it wasn't the same as having a mother. "It's great to have a whole family again."

As Kelly finished speaking, she glanced in Brent's direction. She was startled by the hurt look on his face.

Brent noticed her curious gaze and recovered quickly. Giving her a big smile, he turned the subject back to their plans for the evening. Within moments the bell rang, and they all jumped up to head to their next class.

Greg gave Kelly's hand a warm squeeze and then headed down the hallway. He had also seen the look on Brent's face. There had been such naked hurt there. What had caused it? Had it been Kelly's talk about Peggy and her family? Greg didn't really know much about his friend's family except that Brent's father had left them for another woman. Brent never talked about it. Greg had met Brent's mother at the Thanksgiving picnic a couple of weeks ago. He had liked her but had noticed that she seemed to be in her own world most of the time. What was it like at Brent's house? he wondered.

TWO

C-r-y-y-y-s-t-a-a-l!" Kelly ducked her head back in the car window to escape the cold rushing wind after she yelled for her filly.

"S-h-a-a-a-n-d-y!" Greg braved the cold longer than Kelly. Watching the pasture intently, he didn't pull his head in and roll up the window until he saw the muscular form of his buckskin gelding burst from the woods and race toward the pasture gate. Flying right beside him was Kelly's beautiful, coal-black filly, Crystal. The two horses were fast friends and inseparable in the pasture. Where one was you would always find the other.

Julie laughed in admiration as the beautiful horses skimmed across the field. "They sure do love you a lot. It must be neat to have horses that run to you when you call them."

"Yeah, well we're not sure whether they're nuts about us or the carrots and apples they always know we'll have for them." Greg gave her a wry smile. "I imagine it's a combination of both."

Kelly laughingly protested, "Hey, speak for yourself. My horse loves me even without the carrots. No animal could resist the amount of love I have for her. She *has* to love me because I love her so much!" She tossed her coppery curls as everyone laughed.

"That's kind of the way I feel about my relationship with Jesus," Peggy commented. "How in the world can I not love someone who loves me so much? The times I've tried to walk away from him, it's always been his love that has brought me back."

Four heads nodded in agreement as the car rolled to a stop in the parking lot of Porter's Stables. Kelly looked around in satisfaction. The grayness of the day added to the distinction of the barns. Their weathered gray wood was just a shade darker than the color of the sky. The dark outlines of doors and windows brought life to the picture. As usual, everything was spotlessly clean and orderly. If Kelly hadn't known it was real, she would have thought she was staring at a black-and-white photograph. Sudden movement at the gate shattered the stillness of the scene.

Simultaneously, two heads, one a gleaming buckskin, the other a glistening black, appeared over the wooden gate. Seeing Kelly and Greg still sitting in the car, they bobbed their heads and nickered impatiently. Everyone laughed as Kelly and Greg jumped obligingly from the car and walked over to hand out the demanded treats. Brent and Julie were right beside them.

"Greg's dad will be by at five-thirty to pick you guys up," Peggy called from the car. "Dinner will be ready at six. Be late and you'll go hungry."

The four laughed at Peggy's mockingly fierce tone and waved as she drove out of the drive. Giving

Crystal and Shandy a final pat, they turned toward the barn.

"We'll be right back, boy," Greg said to his gelding. "We've got to get your halters and lead ropes as well as get these two amateurs started with their horses."

"Just because we're amateurs doesn't mean you have to point it out to us," Julie protested. "It's going to become glaringly obvious when we get on to ride beside you two."

Kelly laughed but tried to be encouraging. "Hey, we're just here to have fun. I think it's great that Granddaddy is going to let you two ride a couple of the class horses. He's pretty strict about that. With reason, of course. If too many people who don't know what they're doing ride them, they can mess them up for classes."

"We might be amateurs, but at least we know a little," Brent spoke quickly. "I'm sure I could never ride like you and Greg, but I have fun anyway. That is, if you can have fun when you're freezing to death! How cold is it, anyway?"

Kelly did a little dance into the barn as she said, "Thirty-one degrees! And the sky is gray and thick! I told you it was going to snow. How could it not? It will never get a better chance than this. You just watch. I bet we ride in snow this afternoon."

Looking up at the sky before they moved into the barn, the other three were forced to agree.

"The conditions are perfect, all right. I want it to snow as much as you, Kelly. I've always dreamed of riding in the snow but have never had the chance." Greg's voice was expectant.

It took only minutes for Greg and Kelly to bridle and saddle Shandy and Crystal. Leaving their horses cross-tied in the barn aisle, they turned to help Brent and Julie tack their horses.

"Granddaddy was great to let you have Jackson and Ralph." Kelly tightened the girth on Julie's horse as she spoke. "They can be hardheaded in class, but they love going on the trails and always behave. Besides that, their gaits are really smooth so they won't beat you to death. I think you'll like them."

Julie nodded. "Whatever you say. I don't think I know the difference between smooth and rough gaits, but I'll take your word about my liking Jackson's."

Greg laughed. "You'd know the difference if you *were* on a horse with rough gaits. You'd spend all your time trying to keep from bouncing all over the saddle or falling off. If you're an experienced rider, a horse with rough gaits is not much fun, but they're bearable. For a beginner, it's no fun at all. I'm with Kelly. I think you'll like these guys." Giving Ralph a final pat, he handed the reins to Brent and walked up to unhook Shandy. "Let's go! If we're going to get to ride in the snow, I want to get started!"

Brent walked out of the barn with his big, bay gelding, shaking his head and laughing. "You're getting as bad as Kelly. It's not snowing *yet*, you know. It could just be a false warning. We haven't gotten hardly any snow around here for the last few years. And it always comes in January or February."

Kelly snorted. "Ye of little faith. I can hardly wait to say I told you so!"

Laughing, the four mounted their horses and headed them toward the woods. Shandy and Crystal were obviously ready for a good time. As soon as Greg and Kelly hit the saddles, they began to dance and prance. Bobbing their heads, they made it known they were primed for action. Ralph and Jackson merely looked on with amused indifference, as if saying that working horses had a more serious outlook on life. They had no interest in making such fools of themselves. It was a good thing, too, since Brent and Julie wouldn't have been able to handle them.

Entering the woods, Kelly was once more reminded of a black-and-white photograph. The muted grays, browns, and blacks of the woods seemed to be swallowed in the grayness of the sky. The air was still and silent. No movement marred the perfection of the winter scene. The heaviness of the embracing cold swallowed their chatter. For the next few minutes, the only sound was the horses' even walk. This was a time for thinking and feeling.

Greg was the one to break the contemplative mood. "My body is going to freeze to the saddle if we don't move beyond a walk. I need to get some blood circulating!" Loosening the reins a little, he urged Shandy into a brisk trot.

The woods became a place of life once more as the four horses surged forward, moving single file down the trail toward the large pasture on the far side of the farm.

Kelly observed Julie and Brent carefully for a few minutes. She had been responsible for Granddaddy's allowing them to use the horses, and he had put her in charge. Even though they were bouncing around a little bit, she was satisfied that they were using their legs and not relying on their mounts' mouths for balance. She relaxed her vigil and settled down to enjoy Crystal.

She fell more in love with her black filly every day. In all truth, Crystal wasn't really a filly anymore. At three-and-a-half, she had reached the mare stage, but she still acted so much like a kid that Kelly felt justified in calling her a filly. Kelly reached down to pat her neck. Stroking the fur, she laughed at the thick coat Crystal had grown. "You're more like a big, black bear than a horse right now. If thick fur is any indication of a snowy winter, we're due one for sure."

Julie, just in front of Kelly, overheard her quiet comment and turned to grin over her shoulder. "They all kind of look like woolly bears. As cold as it is, though, I know *I'd* want to have all this fur!"

They broke out of the woods. Glancing up, Kelly thought the sky looked even thicker and closer than it had just minutes before. Surely . . .

Just then, wafting down from the sky, as if not sure it should beat all its friends to the ground, came one lone snowflake. Kelly whooped in delight as she reached out to catch the delinquent flake on her glove. A sudden flurry of swirling crystals rushed to the aid of their captured friend. Kelly's laughter was echoed by Greg, Brent, and Julie as they all lifted their faces to the first snowfall of the year. Sitting still on their expectant horses, the group was suddenly curtained off from the world by the flying flakes.

"Hey, what is this?" Greg's voice sounded a little startled. "Maybe we should head back."

Kelly laughed. "Not on your life! The flakes are too big for this to be a serious storm. It's going to blanket us for a while and then let up. This is the best kind of snow to ride in. The ground is still clear, and we can have the fun of riding through it. Let's go!" Leaning forward, she let Crystal break into the canter she had been asking for for the last few minutes.

She heard the other three whoop in agreement and open their horses up to follow her. Kelly knew Crystal wanted to take off and fly, but she wasn't going to risk Brent's and Julie's safety. They weren't experienced enough to do mad dashes across the pasture. Besides, she was having fun this way. Reining Crystal in just a little, she waited until the four were riding side by side. Exchanging delighted looks with Julie, she turned her face up to the snow and reveled in its fluffy whiteness.

Their calls filled the air and bounced off the wall of snow surrounding them. There was enough visibility for safety, but they still felt as if they were encased in their own little world. It was just them and four pounding horses. Looming in front of them was the guardian oak of the pasture. Greg led the way under its sheltering arms and pulled Shandy to a stop. Snow still flurried around them, but the massive trunk was sheltering them from the wind and the blowing cold.

"Whew! Even with all this exercise I feel like my feet are frozen! The fire at your house tonight is going to feel mighty good, I think." Greg rubbed his hands together as he spoke.

"I'm with you," Brent agreed. "At least in soccer you keep moving enough to stay warm. I'm having a blast, but I sure am cold. I thought three layers would take care of it—next time I'll wear more!" Brent flapped his arms in an effort to get warm but stopped quickly when Jackson began to move restlessly under him. "Guess he doesn't think much of a big bird riding him."

"Not one that looks like you!"

"Hey, woman! Watch your tongue, or I'll have to cream you in Pictionary tonight."

Julie merely laughed at his words. "You guys don't stand a chance of beating us girls. We have a special ability to communicate that you guys can only dream about!"

Brent and Greg snorted.

"Look. It's starting to slacken off." Kelly drew their attention back to the snow. "I didn't think it would last long. And look at the time! Greg, your dad is going to be here in forty-five minutes. We better get going." Moving off at a fast trot, she headed toward the woods. Cocking her head back to listen, she knew the other three were following her.

• • •

"Goodbye, Mr. Adams!" Four voices raised in unison as Greg's father stepped from the car and let Greg slide in behind the wheel. "Thanks for picking us up!"

"You're welcome. Have fun tonight." Turning to Greg, he said, "See you by midnight."

"Okay, Dad. Thanks for letting me have the car."

Minutes later the four pulled up in front of Kelly's house. The car's heater had done a fairly good job of warming them, but everyone was eager for hot food and a chance to plop down in front of the fireplace. Piling from the car, they raced for the kitchen door. Leading the way, Greg burst in the back entrance. Feeling just as much at home in Kelly's house as he did in his own, he grabbed Kelly's twelve-year-old sister, Emily, by the waist and swung her around.

Laughing, Peggy turned from the stove where she was standing. "A little excited by the snow, are we?"

Kelly bobbed her head up and down. "You should have been out there, Peggy. It started snowing while we were in the pasture. It was great!" Grabbing a corn muffin, she sat down on the stool by the counter.

Julie sank down next to her. "Chili! And corn-bread! How did you know that's what I was dying for? There's nothing that takes care of a cold stomach better than chili."

"You can say that again! I'm starving." Brent made a pitiful face and sidled up to put an arm around Peggy.

She waved a spoon playfully in the air and started to say something but was interrupted by Kelly's dad, Scott Marshall, appearing at the base of the stairs. "Do I see a strange man with his arm around my wife in my house? You can't be too hungry. Do you really expect me to let you eat here after getting fresh with my wife?" Laughter rang through the kitchen as the bantering and playing around continued.

Finally, Peggy resumed control. "If everyone is really hungry, then you can all help. Kelly, you and

Julie fix the drinks. Greg, you know where everything is. You and Brent can set the table. Emily, why don't you dish up salad for everyone? And Scott, why don't you make sure the fire is all ready to light when we're done in here?"

Within minutes they were all seated around the table. The hungry crew easily demolished the huge pot of chili Peggy had made. The last crumbs of cornbread were polished off, and there was not even any salad left.

Greg leaned back against his chair with a sigh. "Thanks, Peggy. I feel like a new man. There's something about being in the snow that gives a person an incredible appetite."

"Not that you don't always eat like a horse anyway," Emily teased.

"He's a growing boy, Em. He needs his nourishment."

Greg nodded and smiled at Peggy for coming to his defense.

Kelly rose from the table and pulled down a container off of the refrigerator. Lifting the top, she grinned at the exclamations of delight.

"Chocolate cake!" Brent said. "My favorite. I think I've died and gone to heaven. I haven't eaten a meal like this in so long, I can't even remember the last one."

Kelly and Greg exchanged glances. Did Brent's mom not cook meals? It was obvious he was having a wonderful time, but his comment and his face seemed to betray a hunger and a longing. Greg resolved then to find out what he could from Brent about his family.

• • •

After dinner the entire group collapsed in front of the television. Peggy and Scott claimed places on the sofa while Kelly, her friends, and Emily settled for huge pillows on the floor. Scott had touched off a huge blaze in the fireplace as they entered the room. Its licking flames were already casting a cozy warmth.

Two hours later, Greg reached up to turn off the television and eject the tape from the VCR. "What a great movie. I've seen *White Christmas* at least a dozen times, but I never get tired of it. It's a tradition in my family, too, to start the Christmas season with this movie."

Peggy yawned and stretched from her seat on the sofa. "I'm ready for bed! Y'all can have the place to yourselves for Pictionary. Just try to keep it down to a low roar."

"I think I'll join you," Scott said as he stifled a yawn.

"Bed sounds good to me, too," Emily added. "You girls will just have to win without me."

"Goodnight, you guys," Kelly said as her parents and Emily headed for the stairs. "Oh, and Peggy, thanks again for dinner. It was great!"

"You're welcome," Peggy smiled. "What time do you have to be up in the morning? You might need some encouragement to climb out of a warm bed."

"I guess I need to be up by seven since my first class starts at nine. It's going to be freezing out there tomorrow," Kelly sighed. "I think I'd rather be riding one of the horses than just standing there yelling instructions. But I'm not complaining. Maybe we'll get more snow tomorrow."

"You might just luck out," her father called as he climbed the stairs. "The weatherman says we could get some accumulation tomorrow. Time will tell."

• • •

Greg gave Brent a grin as he returned to the car after walking Julie to her front door and seeing her in. "Fun night."

"You bet it was," Brent nodded. "The Marshalls are really cool people. I had a great time—even if the girls did beat us at Pictionary, like they predicted."

"Yeah, well, we'll get them next time."

Silence fell for a few moments while Greg tried to figure out how to bring up the subject of Brent's family.

Brent took care of it for him. "It's hard to imagine Kelly and Peggy ever had problems. They seem to be so close. Their whole family seems to have so much fun. She's pretty lucky."

Brent tried to speak casually, but Greg could detect a wistfulness in his voice. He decided he couldn't have a better opening than this one.

"Kelly and Peggy have come a long way. Once Kelly became a Christian, things got a lot better, but it wasn't until she let go of all the hurt from her mother's death and let the walls down that things got really good. Family stuff can be hard to work out sometimes." Pausing, he tried to keep his voice light, "So what's your family like, Brent?"

Greg sensed, rather than felt, Brent stiffen beside him. "My family? Oh, it's just a family. It's fine, I guess. My mom and I get along okay."

Greg tried again. "That's cool. What about your dad? What's it like with him not there?"

Brent's laugh was forced this time. "Oh, it's no big deal. Lots of kids don't have their fathers around. But hey, you'll get to meet him next Friday. We're going to have a great time in D.C."

Greg knew he wasn't going to find out anything after Brent began to ramble about what they were going to do in Washington, D.C. It was obvious Brent didn't want to talk about his family. But it was just as obvious that he was unhappy with the situation. All Greg knew to do was wait and hope that sometime his friend would want to talk about it.

THREE

Greg groaned when his alarm went off the next morning at seven. Reaching out to turn off the offending noise, he snatched his arm back under the warmth of the heavy comforter on his bed. It was Saturday, he thought to himself. Why in the world was he getting up so early? Forcing his brain to focus, he stared out at the cold, gray morning unfolding outside his window. The weatherman just might be right this time. The sky definitely looked like it wanted to dump a heavy load of snow.

Greg's mind turned to the fun he had had yesterday riding Shandy in the snow. Shandy. Horses. Kelly. That was it! he suddenly realized. He was supposed to teach Kelly's riding lessons this morning so she could cover for Mandy, the stable trainer and her good friend, in the advanced ring. But what a day to be teaching outside. It couldn't be more than twenty-five degrees, he guessed. Hauling himself up on one elbow, he peered through the frost on his window at the thermometer stationed just outside. Great. Twenty-four degrees! Groaning again, he threw his legs outside the covers, took a deep breath, and dashed for the shower. It was on mornings like this that he paid for the fact he liked to sleep in a cold room.

Emerging twenty minutes later, he dug through his drawers and came up with what he hoped were enough layers to keep warm. Starting with a layer of insulated underclothes, he added flannel-lined jeans, two pairs of thick wool socks, a turtleneck, and a thick wool sweater. He pulled out his lined jean jacket to top it off. A thick wool hat and lined leather gloves were stuffed in his pockets before he clambered downstairs for breakfast.

● ● ●

Kelly looked up from brushing Crystal as Greg walked in the barn. "Looks like you've gained about ten pounds since last night," she teased.

"I could say the same about you, but women always get insulted if you talk about their weight." Greg's voice was just as cheerful. A huge mound of pancakes and five strips of bacon had done much to improve his outlook on life.

Kelly laughed. "Since it's only temporary, I guess I can take the insult. I started out with a ton of layers, and then Dad gave me his coveralls to add to it. I realize I probably look weird, but I'm warm. And in this weather that's quite an accomplishment."

"You got that right! Do you really think any students will actually show up? Don't they know they're going to freeze to death if they sit on top of a horse for an hour?"

"Oh, the ones who are like me will show. There didn't used to be anything that could keep me from riding. If I was only going to ride one day of the week, I wasn't about to miss it." Kelly finished brushing Crystal and slipped her another carrot before leading her to her stall. "There you go, girl," she said to her beloved filly. "We'll go for a ride after lunch."

Greg grabbed his bucket of brushes and moved into Shandy's stall. "It's warmer in here, old boy, so here we are going to stay. You can enjoy hay while I give you your morning beauty treatment."

Kelly moved toward the tack room. "Granddaddy brought us out a big thermos of hot chocolate. He said he would keep it filled so we didn't turn into ice cubes out here. It tastes great."

"I'll grab a cup in a few minutes. By the way, how many are supposed to show up in my classes this morning?"

Kelly stopped and leaned against Shandy's door. "Your first class has ten intermediate students, the second class has twelve. You might get half today. I only have five in each of Mandy's advanced classes. I have no idea how many of them will brave the cold." Watching Greg brush Shandy's shining coat, she continued, "I really appreciate you doing this. With Mandy at her brother's wedding, there are a lot of classes and chores to cover."

"I'm glad to do it. I wasn't thrilled when my alarm went off at seven, but it's fun now that I'm here." He threw the brush he was using back in the bucket. "Hey, I'm done with Shandy. He only gets a quick brushing for now. Where did you say that hot chocolate was?"

"Follow me."

"In a minute. Come here."

Kelly turned as Greg walked up behind her.

"I haven't given you a hug today, and you look like a doll in that huge jumpsuit." Wrapping his arms around her, Greg gave her a big hug.

Kelly's heart jumped as she thrilled anew at how much Greg cared for her. Returning his hug, she gazed up and gave him a big smile. Hand in hand they walked to the tack room and settled down on chairs while they drank their steaming cups of cocoa. The time passed quickly as Kelly filled Greg in on what he needed to teach in his classes that morning.

• • •

Kelly hooked her heels under the fence, thankful that the biting north wind was to her back. Only two of Mandy's five students had shown up that morning, but she had been right on target about Greg's first class. Five of Kelly's usual ten had come for their riding lesson.

Leaning forward, Kelly directed her attention to the two young women in the arena. Sometimes she felt funny when she taught people who were older than herself. Her two students today were in their early twenties and had been riding for a little over a year. She knew she was much more experienced than they were, but would they be willing to listen?

"We are going to spend most of our time today at a trot," Kelly began. "I think it will help to keep both you and the horses warm. Posting to the trot uses more energy than any other riding you can do."

Sharon, the taller of the two, smiled at Kelly as she rode by. "That's a great idea. I didn't want to miss my lesson today, but I must admit that I'm freezing. It's colder out here than I thought."

"Yeah," Kelly agreed. "It still hasn't hit thirty degrees, and the north wind has the windchill factor down to almost zero. If you get too miserable, we can take a break and get some hot chocolate. In the meantime, I want you to do a posting trot and warm both your muscles and your horses' muscles up. This would be a great day to strain something."

Kelly watched their form for about ten minutes as the young women and their horses circled the arena. Convinced they were warmed up, she raised her voice to be heard over the wind. "Mandy said she wanted you to work on collecting your animals today. Both of your horses are moving at a good pace, but they are pretty strung out. They will look better and the ride will feel better if you can collect their bodies under you. You can accomplish that by applying more leg pressure to push them forward. I don't want you to pull back on your reins, but I want you to gain, and maintain, contact with their mouths. As your legs push them forward, it will move them forward into the bit. Your hands will keep their heads from pushing forward. Their bodies will be forced to collect underneath them."

Sharon and Beth had pulled their horses to a stop in front of Kelly as she talked because they were having a hard time hearing her over the wind. Their expressions were ones of concentration as they listened intently.

"You definitely know your stuff, Kelly," Beth said as she gathered the reins to move Amber, the sorrel mare she was riding, back to the fence. "How is Crystal doing?"

Kelly's face brightened. "She's doing great! She's really eager to learn and wants to do everything she can to please me. She's coming along really well. Mandy says I can start jumping her next year."

Nodding, Sharon and Beth moved their horses back into a posting trot. For the next thirty minutes they worked hard to coordinate their hands and legs in order to collect their horses. It was difficult to get a true feel for the horses, but both women improved a lot in the brief time they had.

Kelly, in an effort to stay warm, jumped down from the fence and walked around the inside of the arena as she called encouragement and suggestions. She could see Greg doing the same thing in the other arena. Several times they caught each other's eyes and smiled. She could tell by the laughter coming from her intermediate students that they were having a good time. Greg and Kelly had agreed that in honor of the students being brave enough to come out in this cold, they would give them a fun day. Before the students had gotten there, she and Greg had set up an obstacle course with barrels and poles. It included riding and dismounting to run between stations. The kids were having fun, and it was keeping them warm. That was all anybody could ask for on a day like today.

Just as Kelly was getting ready to call Sharon and Beth in to give them the final instructions Mandy had left, the first snowflakes began to fall. Judging from the size of the flakes, Kelly knew this was the snowfall the weatherman had predicted. There was supposed to be five or six inches before it was all over. She made no effort to control the grin spreading across her face.

Sharon laughed at Kelly's expression. "A snow lover, are you?"

"You bet I am! I wouldn't want it all the time, but I think December is made for snow."

"Yeah? Well, I moved from New York just to get away from this stuff. But I must admit I like the first snowfall of the year. At least here I know it won't continue for months at a time. This looks like the real thing," she predicted. "We'll probably have six inches before it stops tonight. Should be great for sledding tomorrow."

Kelly nodded in excitement and then turned as Granddaddy Porter's voice sounded behind her.

"Probably need to call a halt to things, Kelly. This snow is the real thing. I don't want anyone to have trouble trying to get home. The streets will get bad quick. They're so cold that the snow will begin to stick right away. What time are your folks coming after you?"

"Oh, they're not coming till this afternoon," Kelly answered. "I promised Mandy I'd take care of all the barn chores, and I'm going to keep my promise. But it's okay. My dad has a four-wheel-drive truck, so we'll be fine."

Granddaddy nodded in satisfaction and turned away. "I've got some soup on the stove. Why don't you and Greg come get some when you've put the horses away? It'll keep you warm."

"Thanks, Granddaddy. How about if we come in after we ride?"

"You're going riding?"

Kelly nodded vigorously. "I wouldn't miss riding in this snow for the world. It's so much fun! We have plenty of hot chocolate left. We'll tank up before we head out."

"Youngsters!" With that one-word comment, Granddaddy gave a brief nod and headed for his house.

Turning back to Sharon and Beth, Kelly noticed them viewing her with admiration. Sharon spoke, "You're going to have some kind of fun on that black beauty in this snow. I wish I had a camera. More than that, I wish I had my own horse. I'd love to head out in the snow with you."

Kelly smiled as she opened the gate for them to lead their horses through. It took just minutes to untack the horses and let them in the stalls for hay and water. Granddaddy had decided to leave all the horses up today since it was so cold. The barn was cold but at least the animals were protected from the snow and blowing wind.

Greg's class was just finishing up with their horses. With a wave to both Greg and Kelly, his students ran out to their waiting parents.

Kelly turned to Greg with a grin. "Looks like the fun begins!"

He nodded in agreement and reached in to grab Shandy's bridle. "Let's forego the saddles today. I've always wanted to ride bareback in the snow. Besides, it will help keep us a little warmer. I'd rather be in contact with a warm body than a cold leather saddle."

"Sounds good. I'm glad both of our horses have such smooth gaits. Saddle or no saddle—makes no difference to me." Crystal's bridle in hand, Kelly turned toward her filly's stall.

• • •

By the time they emerged from the barn, the snow was falling with a vengeance. Grinning at each other, Greg and Kelly vaulted onto their horses. Moving over to the gate, Kelly waited while Greg carefully opened and closed the gate from Shandy's back. She was still working with Crystal on that. Sometimes Crystal was fine; other times the swinging gate made her nervous and she wouldn't stand still. Shandy was an old hand at it.

Greg looked at Kelly with a question in his eyes. She knew immediately what he was thinking.

"Of course we're headed for the oak pasture," she said with a laugh. "I think a good race would make all of us happy. But first we need to warm their muscles up."

Settling into an easy trot, they moved down the field and into the woods. The snow was turning the woods into a fairyland. Flakes swirled all around them, making the air seem like a living thing. Limbs tossed in the wind, appearing to bat the flakes around, but all in vain. More than they could bat continued to descend. The trees' tossing arms were gradually coated with a white blanket. Ultimately, they would bow to the forces. Resigned to their inevitable fate, the woodland undergrowth was already sporting a thickening cloak of snow.

Moving into the open pasture, Kelly and Greg gave the horses their heads and let them decide the

pace. Crystal and Shandy, still impatient from
the reduced speed of yesterday, tossed their heads
and took off at a dead run. Crouching low to
their horses' necks, both for speed and to protect
their faces from the driving wind, Kelly and Greg
narrowed their eyes to slits and let out yells of happiness. The force of the driving wind made it impossible
to see and steer the horses, so they just settled in to
enjoy the ride.

Kelly and Greg were vaguely aware when the
huge oak flashed by, but neither Shandy nor Crystal
slowed down. The riders were content to let the
horses continue their wild run. Everyone concerned
was having too much fun to bring it to an end.

Finally, the horses began to slacken their speed
and settled down to an easy canter. Puffs of snow
rose from under their hooves as the world continued to swirl with whiteness. Kelly laughed as she
looked at the accumulation of snow on Greg's jacket
and hat.

"Don't laugh too hard," Greg objected. "You look
just as much like a snowman, or I should say woman,
as I do. Even your eyelashes are coated." He looked
at her warmly.

Kelly blushed but met his eyes squarely and
grinned. "Is this fun or what? Even though Crystal
has been mine for three months, it still seems like a
dream half the time that I actually own such an
incredible animal. I keep thinking I'll wake up and
find out it wasn't real."

"She's real all right, Kelly. And just as beautiful as
you are."

Kelly blushed again. She didn't know if she would
ever get used to Greg complimenting her. She kind

of hoped not. She liked the thrill that coursed through her body when he looked at her like that. "Thanks." She wished she could think of something more to say, but nothing would come.

Reaching down to pat Crystal's neck, Kelly's thoughts returned to her responsibilities. "Crystal is pretty warm. It's going to take a while to cool the horses off once we get back, and we still have a lot of chores to do. We'd better head toward the barn."

"Whatever you say. You're the boss today." Greg grinned easily and took the lead as he turned Shandy onto the wooded trail and brought him down to a trot.

In just the thirty minutes they had been in the pasture, the woods had been subdued by the snowfall. It lay quietly under its cloak of glistening crystals and seemed resigned to accepting the burden that continued to fall. Indentions left by the horses' hooves were filling in quickly as flakes rushed to remedy the marring of their sanctuary.

• • •

Riding into the sheltered covering of the barn, Kelly and Greg slid off their steaming horses' backs. Quickly trading bridles for halters, they cross-tied Crystal and Shandy and then disappeared once more into the tack room. The next time they emerged, they were carrying thick, warm horse blankets which they promptly put on their mounts.

"I sure am glad we bought these things," Kelly said. "As hot as these guys are, it wouldn't be good for them to cool off too quickly. It may take us a while to get them ready to put up."

"They're both in really good shape," Greg pointed out. "It shouldn't take too long. But we'll definitely give it as long as it takes. After the scare last month with Crystal's colic, I'm not about to take any chances."

Kelly's response was fervent. "You got that right!"

Unhooking their horses, they lapsed into silence as they walked up and down the aisles of the barn. Though the barn was cold, it actually felt kind of warm after the intensity of the wind and snow. With the lights blazing, it was quite cozy. Kelly felt herself relaxing along with Crystal.

Thirty minutes later she was satisfied with her filly's condition and released Crystal into her stall still blanketed. On a night like this, Crystal would enjoy the extra warmth. While Greg gave Shandy another five minutes, Kelly began to scoop feed into the wheelbarrow. Glancing at her watch, she noticed they had just about two hours before her father was due to pick them up—plenty of time to do all the chores if they worked hard.

The next hour passed quickly as Greg and Kelly fed grain, hay, and water to all the horses. Since Mandy wouldn't be back until the following evening, and Granddaddy was planning on letting the horses out in the morning, there needed to be hay in the fields. Kelly knew the truck would never make it through the deepening snow, so she jumped onto the tractor and started it up. They would have to load the hay into the front-end loader and make several trips until all twenty bales were out.

"You're a tractor woman too, huh?" Greg grinned as he jumped up behind her to ride over to the hay barn.

"It's fun! Mandy taught me how to drive it. It's more fun than the truck." Kelly laughed over her shoulder as the tractor plowed through the deepening snow.

It took the rest of their time to load up the hay and then tractor it to the hay racks where they could undo the twine and dump it in. Neither Kelly nor Greg were cold when all their work was finished. Hard labor had done the job of keeping them warm. Giving Crystal and Shandy a final pat, they moved to the door of the barn to wait for Kelly's father.

"You know," Greg said, "I sure could use some of that soup Granddaddy offered us earlier. I'm starving."

Kelly laughed. "I'm hungry, too. We have a couple of minutes, and Dad won't mind coming in and waiting for a little while. Let's go! I think my blood is going to congeal if we just stand here."

Within seconds they were on Granddaddy's porch and ringing the bell.

"Come in, you two!" Granddaddy greeted them with a warm smile. "I've been keeping the soup hot for you. I figured your stomachs would make you pay some attention to them sooner or later."

Greg rubbed his hands in anticipation as he peeled off layers. "Thanks, Granddaddy. I feel like I could eat the whole pot at this point."

It didn't take Greg and Kelly long to polish off the huge bowls of vegetable soup Granddaddy set in front of them. Mopping it up with chunks of homemade bread baked by Granddaddy's daughter, they finally settled back with a sigh. Only then did Kelly look out the window at the drive.

"I wonder where Dad is? He's usually on time. I hope everything is all right."

Granddaddy spoke. "He's probably just a little behind schedule because of the snow. He shouldn't have any trouble with that four-wheeler of his. The snow has knocked out my phone service, so he couldn't call if he wanted to. He'll be here soon."

Kelly nodded and then turned to Greg. "Dad and Peggy are going out tonight, so I told them I would hang out with Emily and her friend who is spending the night. They're going to be on a tight schedule with Dad picking us up late. Why don't we go ahead and get dressed? We can wait outside until he gets here. It'll take a few minutes to put our layers back on."

Greg nodded in agreement and began to reach for his things hanging on the hooks by the front door. "Thanks for the soup, Granddaddy. It was great!"

"Thank *you* for all of y'alls help. I'm just too old to do all that work anymore. A couple of bowls of soup was the least I could do. If you get too cold waiting out there, you can come back in."

Kelly and Greg walked back out into the winter wonderland. Snow was still falling heavily, and a muted hush had fallen over the stables. Even though it was only four in the afternoon, the quiet of the world made it feel much later.

Kelly slipped into her own little world of thought as she listened to the muffled snorts and stomps of the horses in the weathered barn. Her thoughts were ended abruptly when a snowball smashed against her back.

Wheeling around, she glared at Greg's laughing face and then dissolved into laughter herself. Reaching down, she grabbed her own handful of snow. War began.

Dodging behind trees and bushes, the two launched missiles as quickly as they could scoop and pack them. Kelly took more direct hits, but Greg was at a distinct disadvantage. Kelly's coveralls protected her from any snow falling down into her clothes. Greg had no such protection. Laughing, he finally charged her and wrestled her to the ground. She put up a good fight, but she was no match for his size and strength. Gasping for breath, she finally lay quietly.

"Okay, you beast," she said. "You couldn't win fair and square, but you have conquered me by brute strength and size. Does your male ego feel better?"

Greg grinned down at her. "I am vindicated, therefore I am satisfied!" Jumping up, he pulled her to her feet and brushed the majority of the snow off.

Still breathing hard, they took refuge in a sheltered part of Granddaddy's porch. They sat quietly for a few minutes until Kelly turned to Greg.

"Have you noticed the way Brent's been acting lately? It seems like something is bothering him. Do you know what's going on?"

Greg shrugged. "I tried to talk to him last night, but all he did was change the subject. I know his family situation must be bugging him, but he won't talk about it. All I know to do is keep trying. Maybe he'll talk about it one of these days."

Kelly nodded. "Sometimes it's hard to talk about things when you're in the middle of them. It usually helps, though. He must feel like he's pretty alone. Julie called me after you took her home last night. She's concerned about him. She said he's been getting moody a lot lately, but when she tries to talk about it, he laughs and changes the subject."

"Yeah, I recognize that tactic. I guess only time will help us figure out what's going on with him."

FOUR

Greg grabbed Brent as he emerged from church beside his mother. "Hey, man. Are you going sledding with us at the golf course?"

Brent shook his head. "I don't think I can. I didn't hear about the sledding until today, so I didn't bring any lunch. And if I go home to eat, I won't be able to make it back over here. My mom has some plans for the afternoon."

Greg grinned. "No problem! Some people made phone calls last night, but they weren't able to get everyone. I thought there might be some people who didn't come prepared, so I made a few extra sandwiches and grabbed extra cookies from the pile that's been growing at my house this month because of my mom's Christmas baking. After we sled, everyone is headed back to my house for soup and bread. I even brought some extra clothes. What do you say?"

Brent glanced at his mother who nodded. "Have a good time," she said. "Call me when you're ready to come home, and I'll pick you up."

Brent grinned and slapped Greg on the shoulder. "Thanks, buddy. Looks like we're on. Let's go."

Turning, they headed for the group growing in the parking lot. The streets were still too slippery for the bus, but the golf course was only a few blocks away so they were going to walk.

Reaching into his parents' car, Greg grabbed a huge bundle of snow clothing. "Let's go, Brent. The girls are already changing. We only have about ten minutes before we're supposed to leave."

• • •

Kelly hugged her sled tight and grinned at Greg. "This is going to be so much fun! The snow is perfect. The layer of sleet that fell late last night has made it just right for sledding. And tubing. I think I actually like tubing better than sledding. Crashing into people is fun when you're on inner tubes."

Greg regarded her with mock concern and shifted his inner tube to his other hand. "There is a violent side to your personality that I've not noticed until now. First, you tried to annihilate me in a snowball fight, and now you're wanting to crash inner tubes. What else am I going to find out about you?"

Kelly stuck out her tongue but merely laughed. "You'll learn you'd better be careful around me. You never know what to expect!"

Greg laughed. "I've figured that out already. It's part of what makes you so much fun."

Julie and Brent walked up to join them on the slopes. They both were toting big grins and inner tubes.

"Mr. Sorenson just drove up in a truck full of inner tubes," Julie said. "He took them down to the station to blow them up. What a nice man."

Kelly nodded and then headed in the direction of the inner tube pile. "I'm going to abandon my sled for a while. Bumping tubes is too much fun to miss the action. I'll be right back!"

Laying her sled down next to the group gear, she grabbed a tube and headed back to her friends. They had been joined by twenty other kids from the youth group who were equally intent on having fun. Martin was busy lining everyone up in order to start the afternoon with a race. Kelly ran forward to make sure she had a place in the contest. Everyone had abandoned sleds for tubes—for the first run at least.

Lying low on his tube, Brent grinned at Kelly who was bordered by Greg and himself. "Don't look so serious, Kelly. It's going to make it harder to lose."

Kelly snorted, "We'll see who's going to lose!" Then she laughed at her own bravado. "It's actually no surprise that the guys usually win. Once the tubes get going, your bigger size and weight make them go faster." Then she gave a sly smile to Julie who was lined up next to Brent. "But you guys might have some surprises this year. The girls did some strategizing this time. I'd be on my guard, if I were you."

Greg was just turning to her with a question when Martin blew the whistle.

Immediately legs and arms began to push tubes down the steep slope, taking only a moment for them to begin to fly. All the boys were focused and heading straight down. The girls had another idea. Letting loose with war whoops, they leaned hard to make their tubes connect with the guys around them. Reaching out, they grabbed on to the tubes and tried to flip the boys off. Half the guys yelled as they went flying. The other half were hanging off their tubes but trying to regain control. Laughter and screams filled the air as the battle raged on.

Kelly was laughing helplessly as she clung to Greg's tube. She had succeeded in knocking him halfway off, but he was still hanging on and trying to knock her loose. His problem was that if he let go enough to knock her off, he was going to fall off himself. Laughing, he finally resigned himself to their tandem condition and rode it out.

When all was said and done, the two girls who had been designated to be the winners made it to the bottom first. The rest of the girls had done their jobs well. Not one guy had been able to slide unhindered down the hill. Reaching the bottom, Kelly joined the rest of the girls in a victory dance that was soon cut short by a volley of snowballs from the defeated males. War broke out for about twenty minutes, and then one by one they picked up their tubes and turned to trudge up the hill.

The afternoon passed in a haze of fun and laughter. Kelly lost count of the times she and the rest of their foursome climbed to the top of the hill and then whooped in delight as they flew down the slope. As the day wore on and the snow became more and more packed, the hill became faster and faster. The temperature didn't climb out of the lower thirties, and there were a few short snow flurries that kept alive the promise of more snow. When

Kelly and her friends were sure their hands and feet were going to fall off from the cold, they moved over to one of the fires built in the large fifty-five gallon drums set up at the bottom of the hill. Huddling around a drum until their limbs had thawed, they would then head back for more fun. Most of the afternoon was a free-for-all, but Martin also set up several relays for the entire group. When parents started arriving at five to cart people over to Greg's, everyone was ready to call it quits in order to head for warmth and food.

● ● ●

"Thanks." Kelly smiled gratefully as Greg handed her a huge bowl of soup and a generous hunk of homemade bread. "I was already tired, but the combination of the fireplace and this hot chocolate has turned me into an absolute noodle! I just can't seem to make my body work. I'm not sure I could have stood up to go get this."

Julie echoed her sentiments as she reached for the bowl Brent offered her. "The best description of me right now would be a slug. I sure hope this food gives me some energy, or I might be sleeping right here on your floor tonight, Greg. I don't think I can move."

"I know how you feel." Greg sank down beside Kelly. "My hunger pangs were enough to get me off the floor for food, but once I've eaten I don't think I'll be moving either. Thankfully, we don't need to. I feel for Martin, though. He played as hard as we did this afternoon, and he still has to talk tonight."

The other three merely nodded as they attacked the delicious soup parents had fixed and brought over. Kelly quit counting after her third slab of homemade bread, and she didn't even bother to keep track of the cookies she ate. All she knew was that she was full and ready to curl up somewhere for a long winter's nap. She could feel her eyes growing heavy.

"Hey, you. It's not bedtime yet." Greg gently shook Kelly's shoulder. "The night is still young. I think Martin is getting ready to start."

Kelly forced her eyes open and tried to straighten up. Looking over at Julie, she laughed. "You look as tired as I feel. I didn't even see the truck that hit me, but I think it backed up and finished off the job! It's a good thing my dad is coming to pick me up. He may literally have to do that. I really don't think I can move. He'll just have to carry me to the car."

"I hope I can stay awake to hear Martin," Julie sighed. "I can barely keep my eyes open."

Brent laughed as he poked her playfully in the side. "Oh, I'll make sure you stay awake. It won't look good if my girlfriend is falling asleep during the meeting. They'll think I kept you out too late last night or something."

"You *did* keep me out too late last night." Turning, Julie answered the question before Kelly asked it. "We went to a Christmas production with his mom last night. It was at one of the churches in Raleigh—two hours there and two hours back. It was great, but we didn't get home until almost one in the morning, and then I had to get up for church this morning. I think the same truck that hit you came back for me."

Just then Martin made his way to the front of the room and sat down next to the fireplace. "This seems to be the warmest spot in the house, so I'm going to stay right here. I know all of you are tired, so why don't we do something to get your blood moving. I promise not to talk long, but I really want y'all to hear what I have to say." Standing to his feet, he continued, "I want everyone to stand up."

Just that simple command was met with moans and groans.

"Oh, come on, you bunch of couch potatoes," Martin teased. "What happened to all the youthful energy and exuberance I hear about?"

Brent grimaced as he struggled to rise. "I think it died on about the fortieth time up the hill."

Martin laughed but continued to motion them to get up. "I'm still going, and I'm almost twice most of y'alls age. If this old man can stay awake a little while longer, so can you." Looking around the room and seeing everyone standing, he smiled. "Now I want everyone to do twenty jumping jacks. Believe me, you'll feel better."

Groans intensified in volume around the room, and several kids just shook their heads in disbelief. Martin, seemingly oblivious to the mutiny, led the exercises. Kelly was sure he had done close to fifty jumping jacks by the time she managed to complete her twenty, but she had to admit she did feel better. At least she thought she'd be able to keep her eyes open now. Sitting back down on the floor, she leaned against the sofa but kept her back straight. It would be easier to stay awake that way.

It took a few minutes for everyone to settle down, and then Martin opened his Bible. "Everyone turn to the book of James, chapter 1." Flipping the pages, he found what he was looking for. "Look at verses 2-4: 'Consider it pure joy, my brothers, whenever you face trials of many kinds, because you know that the testing of your faith develops perseverance. Perseverance must finish its work so that you may be mature and complete, not lacking anything.'"

Martin paused and looked out at the faces peering up at him. "Somehow some Christians today have gotten the idea that a relationship with Christ is supposed to be an endless joyride. These Christians feel that they are always supposed to be happy and always supposed to be walking in victory over whatever circumstances life is dealing them at that moment. When that doesn't happen, then many decide that this Jesus stuff doesn't work. Or they think they're just not cut out to be a Christian because they're not happy all the time." Martin could tell by the expressions around the room that he was connecting.

"Let me tell you what the truth is. The truth is that you can count on having troubles as long as you're living on this earth. Christians aren't exempt from trouble. I really don't know where people got the idea that this is true. Look at the great people of the Bible. The apostle Paul was beaten, thrown in jail, run out of town, and sick a lot. I think he would agree there was trouble in his life. Was he walking apart from God? Was he messing up? Is that why he was having so much trouble? Hardly! God used all of those troubles to draw Paul closer to himself. He also used them to reach other people with the news about Jesus. James says to consider it pure joy *when* you face trials—not *if*. He's saying you can count on them as long as you're here on earth."

Martin paused for a moment to let his words sink in, and then plowed ahead. "You might be thinking, so if I'm going to have troubles anyway, why bother being a Christian? I believe that's a question all of us ask at some time. And I think it's an okay question to ask. It's only as you ask questions that you find answers. For me, that question is easy. I can either have the choice of walking through my problems alone or with the Lord of the universe. Since God is in control of everything, I would much rather walk through life with him! I tried doing everything on my own for long enough to know that it doesn't work very well. It's a very lonely existence. God longs to walk side by side with us through life."

He looked back down at his Bible. "Look at the rest of these verses. James says that 'the testing of your faith develops perseverance.' And then he says, 'Perseverance must finish its work so that you may be mature and complete, not lacking anything.' Isn't that what all of us long for? To be mature and complete, not lacking anything? I have to tell you that the only way to get to that point is to walk through the trials and troubles that come your way and learn how to lean on Jesus. *And* learn all the things you need to from those troubles. You can try and run from them, or you can accept their place in your life and make the most of them. It's always your choice. Jesus knows what needs to happen in your life to make you into the kind of person you want to be and who he created you to be."

Flipping his Bible to another section, Martin smiled again at the intense faces. "Thanks for staying awake, you guys. The fact that no one is asleep yet tells me that I'm maybe making some sense and hitting some of you where you are."

Greg glanced over at Brent and wanted to yell "Amen!" His friend was hunched forward in serious concentration. Greg could tell he was soaking up every word. Maybe what Martin was saying was going to help him with whatever he was dealing with.

Martin continued, "Some of you may be wondering about troubles that are devastating. What if you get hit by a drunk driver on the way home tonight? What if your parents get a divorce and your dad leaves? Can you really consider such troubles 'pure joy,' like James says we should? It sounds impossible. But I think we need to understand that having joy is not the same thing as what we would consider happiness. Certainly an accident or a divorce would not cause you to jump up and down with glee or have warm fuzzies. It is possible, though, to decide to trust Jesus and know that because he's God, he can bring good things out of it. That's having joy. Romans 8:28 says it best: 'And we know that in all things God works for the good of those who love him, who have been called according to his purpose.'

"'Called according to his purpose.' That's us. If you know Jesus, if you have a relationship with him, you have been called according to his purpose. And Paul says that in all things God works for the good of those who love him. This is the same guy who's sick a lot, who gets thrown in prison, gets beaten. He has learned that Jesus can take all the bad things of his life and bring good out of them. Once you have that knowledge deep in your heart, you can face the hard times with confidence. They'll still hurt, but at least there is hope of good things coming out of them."

Greg continued to watch Brent. It looked as though the tension was fleeing from his body as he mulled over Martin's words. Obviously Brent was in the middle of some big problems. Hopefully, this would be a turning point for him.

Martin closed the meeting with prayer. There was an air of thoughtful quiet as everyone rose to leave. It took only a few minutes to clean up the stray dishes and napkins that had been missed during the first roundup.

"Hey, Greg, can I use your phone?" Brent asked. "I need to call my mom and have her come pick me up. It should only take her a few minutes to get here."

"You bet. Use the phone in my dad's office. It should be quieter there."

"Thanks."

Greg walked outside with Kelly to wait for her father. She looked at him thoughtfully.

"Martin had some really good stuff to say tonight," she said. "I would have laughed at him before. When I was in the middle of everything with Peggy, I never could have believed good would come from it. Now that I'm on the other side, I can see what he means. I also know that trusting Jesus with everything will take a while, but at least I have one experience behind me."

Greg nodded. "I know what you mean. The only way to really learn how to trust Jesus is to walk through hard times with him and see over and over that he'll always be there and he'll always make things work for good. We're kinda young to have had lots of those experiences, but we're learning."

"Yeah," Kelly agreed. "Here comes my dad. I'll see you at school tomorrow."

Greg gave her a warm hug, and then Kelly ran up the hill to where her father was waiting.

Greg turned to go back into his house and noticed Brent walking out. Even in the dim light he could see the anger on his friend's face. What had happened? Moving to intercept him, Greg prayed silently for help. "Is your mom on the way?"

"Yeah." Brent's tight voice spoke of restrained fury.

"What's wrong, man?"

"Wrong? What could be wrong?" Brent made no effort to hide his sarcasm. He laughed bitterly. "Just when I think things might make sense, I learn they never will."

Greg waited for more but nothing else came. "What do you mean?" he finally asked.

Brent wasn't talking anymore, though. Shaking his head, he managed a more lighthearted laugh. "Oh, it's no big deal. My mom should be here in a couple of minutes. You ready for your chemistry quiz tomorrow?"

Brent had closed up again. Greg longed to make him talk, but he was sure it would be no use. Frustrated, Greg allowed Brent to turn the conversation to school.

As he watched Brent and his mom drive away, Greg stood outside in the snow and struggled with his feelings of helplessness. How could he help Brent if he had no idea what was wrong? Why wouldn't Brent talk to him? What was the good of having friends if you didn't let them know what was going on with you? Finally, Greg turned and slowly walked back inside.

FIVE

Kelly and Julie stood with their backs to the bitter wind as they waited with Greg and Brent for Brent's dad. There had been no more snow since the weekend, but the temperatures had stayed cold so there was still snow on the ground. The week of school had flown by, and the boys were on their way to Washington, D.C. Brent's father had picked up their luggage the night before, so all three of them could head straight out of town when school was over.

Kelly looked up at Greg. "I hope you guys have a great time. I've been to D.C. a couple of times, but I've always wanted to go around Christmas. I'd love to see all the lights and the National Christmas Tree. I bet there will be singing everywhere!"

"It's pretty incredible, all right," Brent spoke up. "My mom, dad, and I went there a few years ago. I had a great time. We had lunch at a restaurant in this really posh hotel. I told my dad then that I would love to stay there someday, and he took me seriously. We're staying at the Mayflower. We'll get some postcards to show you this place. It's unbelievable. I don't even want to know how much it costs!"

"If you can't be rich, it's nice to have rich friends!" Greg joked. "I know we won't be able to see everything that's there, but Brent and I are going to fit in as much as we can." Taking Kelly's hand he smiled at her. "What are you and Julie going to do?"

"Like I said, we're going to enjoy the luxury of shopping without having to worry about our boyfriends grabbing us after they've dressed in women's clothing! Then we're going to work on something..."

Greg grinned. "You're being awfully mysterious. What gives?"

"Noneyo." Kelly's voice was playful.

"Noneyo? What the heck does that mean?"

Kelly grinned back at him. "It means it's none yo business! Asking too many questions can spoil surprises, you know."

Brent and Julie joined in Greg's laughter. Just then Brent spotted his father's car turning into the school drive. After quick hugs, the boys jumped into the car and took off. Kelly and Julie waved them out of sight and then headed back to the warmth of the building. Julie's choral practice was getting ready to start. Kelly was going to do homework while she waited for her friend. Then they were going out to the barn for a little while before they went home to do Christmas baking.

• • •

Greg could hardly believe his eyes when he walked into the Mayflower Hotel. His senses were already overloaded by the glimpses of national monuments he had seen as they had driven through the gaily lit capital city. But the Mayflower took his breath away. No wonder it was called the grande dame of Washington hotels. He stood in the lobby with his mouth open as Brent's father explained that a major restoration in the 1980s had uncovered the large skylights he was gaping at. Their magnificence merely mirrored the elegance surrounding him. Spectacular columns and balconies reflected the same ornate gilding and ornamentation of the ceiling. Italianate murals had also been uncovered during the restoration. Luxurious carpeting and an abundance of marble completed the spectacular scene.

Brent's father checked them in and then led them toward the Cafe Promenade. "I'll let you have a peek before we head for our room. We can put our stuff away and then come back down for dinner."

Brent took one look and whistled. "We're eating in *there*? What bank did you rob, Dad?"

His father just laughed. "It's been a long time since I took you anywhere special. I decided to do it up right."

Brent just shook his head, and Greg detected a sudden tenseness.

Their pink and beige room was just as spectacular as the rest of the hotel. It sported a high ceiling, crown moldings, elegant Federal-style furnishings, marble vanities and elegant bathroom facilities. Greg was overwhelmed by a feeling of instant wealth. His family, when they traveled, usually stayed in the interstate economy hotels. They were fine, but this was something else!

"The guy who designed this place also designed New York City's Grand Central Terminal." Brent's father continued to fill them in about the Mayflower while they quickly unpacked their bags. "And every president since Calvin Coolidge has held his inaugural ball in the Grand Ballroom here. Roosevelt actually lived here during the time between his election and his inauguration. It would be impossible to list all the famous people who have stayed here as guests."

"How far are we from the mall, Dad?" Brent put away the last few things from his bag and moved toward the window.

"Only about a ten-minute walk. We're on Connecticut Avenue. You can walk down 18th and come out right at the Lincoln Memorial. We'll do that in the morning and then work our way up the mall." Grabbing the key, he stuffed it in his pocket. "Let's go, guys. I don't know about you, but I'm starving!"

The boys needed no encouragement to follow him down the hallway to the elevator. A short ride landed them close to the Cafe Promenade. In minutes they were seated under the beautiful domed skylight which had been another discovery during the restoration. Murals, crystal chandeliers, trees, marble columns, and elegant Christmas decorations added to the fairyland world Greg felt he had been thrown into. This was definitely a style of living he had never experienced. He was a little nervous that he would do something wrong, but Brent's dad set him quickly at ease. Greg liked Mr. Jackson instantly. Brent's earlier tension had disappeared, too. He seemed to be having a wonderful time.

"Don't even look at the prices, Greg." Mr. Jackson said. "This weekend is my treat. I want you to order whatever you want."

It didn't take long for the boys to settle on huge slices of rare prime rib. The hot homemade bread, salad, and delicately flavored new potatoes made it an incredible meal. Greg and Brent were both stuffed when they finished, but it didn't take much to talk them into thick slices of creamy cheesecake covered with a generous layer of Ghiradelli chocolate. They could barely move when they pushed back from the table.

"Thanks, Mr. Jackson. I think that's the best meal I've ever had in my life," Greg said. "And I know I've never eaten in such an incredible place. I really appreciate it." Brent echoed his sentiments.

"It's only nine, boys. Are you two up for a walk? It might do you some good after eating so much. The Lincoln Memorial is absolutely beautiful at night. I'd hate to bring you to Washington and not have you see it. It's impressive during the daytime, too, but..."

Greg and Brent exchanged looks and nodded at the same time. Brent answered for them. "Let's do it, Dad. I'm up for maxing out this weekend. We can sleep and lay around when we get home."

Brent's dad grinned. "I was hoping you would feel that way."

• • •

Kelly looked up from her books as Julie came clattering down the stairs after choral practice. Glancing out the window, she saw Julie's mother pull in the school drive.

"Good timing. Here comes your mom. How did practice go today?"

"Really well! Mrs. Marrs says we sound great. There are still a few kinks to work out in some of the songs, but they're coming along. She says we'll be ready for the big night."

Grabbing the book bag she had left on the bench next to Kelly, Julie turned to join her friend who was heading for the door. Ten minutes later Julie's mom was depositing them in the parking lot at Porter's. Just as they stepped from the car, a soft, cold rain began to fall.

"Rain!" Julie wailed. "A few more degrees and all of this would be glorious snow. What good is rain? This *would* have to happen when I get an afternoon to come out."

Kelly wrinkled her nose in agreement but tried to be philosophical. "We'll just have to go to Plan B. Crystal's tack could use cleaning, and I've been wanting to try out the new swing Mandy installed in the hay barn. A rainy afternoon sounds like the perfect time to do that. Cheer up, Julie. We're still going to have a lot of fun."

Julie nodded glumly yet managed a forced smile. Forty-five minutes later her mood had improved immensely.

Rubbing saddle soap carefully into the seat of Kelly's English saddle, Julie grinned at her friend. "This really *is* fun. It's cozy in here. The heater feels great, and all the leather smell is kind of like a perfume. I never knew a tack room could be such a nice place. With the sound of the rain on the tin roof, I could curl up and go to sleep. I'm glad you have the music going. It's helping to keep me awake."

Kelly nodded and reached over to flip the tape of various Christian singers that Peggy had bought for her the week before. "I like all of these, but I still think Amy Grant and Michael W. Smith are my favorites. Peggy has been adding a tape a week to my collection. It's been great to get to know some new singers and groups." Music filled the room again as she continued to rub neat's-foot oil into the soft leather of Crystal's bridle. "It's hard for me to find time to take good care of Crystal's tack, so I'm sometimes thankful for a rainy day. Especially a cold, rainy day. Even Crystal didn't bother me to go for a ride. She seemed quite content to be groomed and then escorted back to her stall. This is definitely a day that's meant for being inside."

"Of course, inside could mean the inside of a hay barn."

Both Kelly and Julie glanced up at the sound of Mandy's voice as she strode through the door of the tack room.

Grinning, Kelly replied, "I think the inside of a hay barn would be a *very* nice place to be. We're almost done here. Are you still up for sharing your new recreational device with us?"

"You bet!" Mandy enthusiastically replied. "This is a perfect day for swinging in the hay barn. And Granddaddy just got a load of hay in yesterday. We can start from really high up."

Julie rubbed faster on the saddle. "I've got all the saddle soap off. I just have to apply the neat's-foot oil. The swing sounds great."

Mandy nodded. "The more the merrier. The saddle should only take you another fifteen minutes or so. I'm going to get the feed ready to go, and then I'll be back." Turning, she disappeared into the barn.

• • •

Kelly rubbed her hands in anticipation when she saw the swing Mandy had rigged in the hay barn. Thick sturdy rope was securely attached to a heavy rubber tire. The entire contraption was suspended from the highest rafter in the barn.

Julie spoke Kelly's thoughts. "How'd you get that thing up there?"

Mandy laughed. "It was every bit as hard as it looks. A couple of my guy friends came over this week. We found the hugest extension ladder we could, and one of them risked his life to climb up there. I can't say it was the sturdiest support in the world, but Jack and I held it steady for him. I can assure you he was glad to get his feet back on the ground! But we had so much fun that night he agreed it had been worth it."

Kelly ran forward to scramble up the stack of hay. "Well, I'm ready to check it out! What do I do?"

Mandy moved over to the swing and gave instructions. "There's a rope tied to the pole behind you. Throw the loose end down to me. I'll tie it around the tire, and then you can haul it up. It's a lot easier than trying to hold it while you climb. Once you get the tire up there with you, simply untie it and fly when you're ready."

Julie climbed up to join Kelly while she was hauling up the tire. Glancing around the barn, Julie remembered Mandy had said that Granddaddy Porter had just gotten in a load of hay. The whole barn was full of the sweet-smelling grass, except for the area in front which he never used and was now taken over by the swing. This was even better than the tack room. Who cared if it rained? Julie thought. Porter's Stables was fun no matter what the weather.

Once Kelly had hauled the tire up, she untied the haul rope and carefully swung her legs over the tire. Inching out to the edge of the stack of hay bales, she grabbed the rope tightly. Giving a push with her feet, she sailed into the air. Julie grinned as she watched her friend go flying down and then soar high into an arc. Back and forth Kelly went with loud yells and calls.

"This thing is great! I mean *great!* Let it rain. Who cares?" Kelly's coppery curls were flying. When she swung to a gentle stop, her blue eyes were glowing. "Mandy, this thing is awesome."

"Yeah, it turned out pretty good, didn't it? Let's give Julie a turn, and then I'm ready for some fun of my own. The only thing Granddaddy has asked is that no one swings on it by themselves. He doesn't want anyone to get hurt, which I can understand." Catching the haul rope Julie tossed to her, she tied it securely and then climbed up to join Julie. Kelly would be in charge of sending the tire up next.

For the next hour the hay barn resembled a huge playground. Once they had gotten their fill of swinging, Kelly convinced Julie and Mandy to build a cavern in the hay stack. Moving hay bales carefully, they ran a tunnel through the stack and then fashioned their own room under the grassy mountain.

Once they had created their chamber, it was as if they were in a world of their own. The hay absorbed all of the outside noise with the exception of the very gentle patter of continuing rain.

Snuggling down into the hay, the three girls relaxed and talked the rest of the afternoon away.

"The boys can have D.C. This afternoon has been really fun." Julie's voice was completely content.

Kelly nodded drowsily. "Yeah, I'd rather be here than fighting D.C. traffic on a Friday afternoon. Maybe I'm turning into a slug, but it sure feels good to just lay around."

Mandy agreed. "This rain is really a blessing. I just wasn't in the mood for giving private lessons this afternoon. This week has been crazy trying to catch up on everything since I was gone last weekend. Being a couch potato can be nice sometimes."

All three girls laid there in silence for a while and then just chatted about nothing of any consequence. Kelly finally looked at her watch and stretched.

"Time to leave our magic world of sweet-smelling hay," she announced. "My dad should be here in about ten minutes. I promised Crystal a couple more carrots before I left for the night."

Minutes later they were standing in the barn. Mandy disappeared down the aisle with the wheelbarrow of feed while Kelly fished carrots out of her locker. "At least these babies stay nice and fresh in here. Who needs a refrigerator in this weather?"

Walking down to Crystal's stall, Kelly wrapped her arms around the filly's neck and absorbed the warmth radiating from her massive form. Crystal nickered and nudged her gently before she began to inspect her pockets.

"Remembered my promise, did you? I'm glad you trust me not to forget." She let Crystal nose around for a few moments before she produced the expected treat. Just as the filly finished the last carrot, Kelly heard her father's car drive up.

• • •

Greg stood in silent tribute before the majesty of the Lincoln Memorial. He had expected something great, but he had not been prepared for its impact on him. He gazed quietly at the hundred-foot rectangular temple perched at the top of the steep stairs. Its white marble glowed softly under the full moon illuminating the city, but it was the artificially lighted statue of Lincoln inside that demanded his attention.

"Many people consider this to be one of the great sculptures of the world," Brent's father spoke quietly beside him. "Stone carvers worked for four years to carve the statue from twenty blocks of Georgia marble."

Greg nodded as he contemplated the figure of Lincoln seated in a high-back chair, grasping its arms, with a slightly downcast look on his face. Greg could almost feel this man's agony as he faced being the president of a nation torn by civil war. It had all just been history from a book to Greg before. Now it seemed to take on life and become a living, breathing reality.

"Let's go up."

Greg, still silent, nodded and followed Brent up the steps. Once inside, he took time to read the two inscriptions engraved on the interior limestone walls of the monument—the Gettysburg Address and Lincoln's Second Inaugural Address. Greg again had the feeling of history coming to life. He turned back to inspect the statue from his closer viewpoint and finally spoke. "This place is really something. I don't think I expected it to have such an impact on me."

"I think all Americans need to come to Washington, D.C.," Brent's father said. "There is no better way to develop a pride in our country than to experience the city where so much of our nation has been formed. Why don't we take a walk down the mall and circle around to our hotel? It's beautiful at night."

Turning, they faced the long reflecting pool in front of the monument. Greg gazed quietly at the tranquility and peace of the pool reflecting both the Washington Monument and the Capitol. He knew he would never forget this night.

Quietly, as if paying respect to all that had come before to make this night possible, Greg, Brent, and Mr. Jackson walked up the mall—past the Vietnam Memorial, under the towering Washington Monument, past the collection of museums Greg was eager to explore the next day. Stopping to look up at the Capitol building, they finally turned and headed back for the Mayflower.

Only when they were a few blocks from the hotel did Greg realize how cold he was. Looking at his watch, he realized it was almost midnight. A nearby marquee revealed that the temperature was just twenty-two degrees, but at least the wind wasn't blowing anymore. The night was still and quiet—as quiet as the bustling city of D.C. got at night. And there were no huge crowds. Greg was glad his first taste of the city had been at night under a full moon.

Glancing over at Brent and his father walking side by side, Greg was satisfied with the look of happiness he saw on his friend's face. Brent seemed to have laid whatever was bothering him aside . . . for now.

• • •

Once the kitchen had been cleaned after dinner, the girls' Friday night project started with a vengeance. Peggy pulled out recipe cards and cookbooks while Kelly, Julie, and Emily pulled out all the standard cookie ingredients they could think of. Once everything was assembled on the counter, Peggy issued instructions.

"Okay, each of us has fifteen minutes to decide what cookies we want to bake tonight. We'll probably have time for two recipes apiece. Once you've decided, you can set up your own station with bowls and everything else you need. Everyone will work from the community supply of ingredients. I stocked up with everything I could think of today, so there should be plenty. If we run out of anything, Scott has agreed to make emergency runs to the store. Once the cookies have cooled, we'll pack them into gift boxes—not to mention eating until we're sick along the way."

Though Peggy flipped through the books with the girls, Kelly knew she had already made up her mind. Peggy would fix Russian Teacakes and Orange Balls. Kelly finally decided to make an old favorite, Congo Squares, and to try a new one. After much flipping she chose Date-Nut Balls. They looked easy but delicious. Julie's and Emily's search netted four more cookie recipes—Almond Fingers, Old Fashioned Sugar Cookies, Lizzies, and Seven-Layer Squares.

Within a few minutes the stations had been set up and the baking had begun in earnest. Scott had to make only one trip to the store for a can of sweetened condensed milk. Kelly knew Peggy had chosen simple recipes so that she could help the three of them, especially Emily, with their cookies. When her father returned with the milk, he stood around with puppy-dog eyes, hoping for a taste of some dough. But they advanced on him with waving spoons until he laughingly retreated.

"There will be no tasting until everyone has a sheet or pan out of the oven." Peggy was adamant. "We'll do the taste test when all recipes are available."

The kitchen rang with laughter and talk as they measured, sifted, stirred, shaped, and poured. Peggy had set up a tape player in the kitchen, and Christmas music poured forth from the speakers. Kelly's heart was content as she paused long enough to gaze around the kitchen. This was the way Christmas was supposed to be. Her mom had done this type of thing before she had gotten cancer. She caught Peggy watching her and flashed her a happy smile.

Scott Marshall walked into the kitchen for what had to have been the tenth time. "How long are you going to make a starving man suffer?" he asked with a pitiful look on his face.

Peggy smiled at him but remained firm. "I told you, no tasting until the first batch of everything is done."

The buzzer on the oven sounded, and Kelly moved over to inspect the tray of sugar cookies baking. "They're perfect, Peggy." Opening the door, she pulled the tray out and laid it on the counter. "That's the last sheet of the first batch." She laughed as her father's face lit up with delight.

"That's my cue!" Rubbing his hands in anticipation, he started forward.

His advance was halted by his laughing wife. "Ten more minutes, love. These babies have to cool before we can decorate them. Emily is finishing up the frosting now. Go back to your recliner and read some more of your book. In ten minutes we'll put you out of your misery."

Grumbling good-naturedly, Scott lowered his head and retreated to the den. Exactly ten minutes later he reappeared and moved toward the counter with a determined look that said nobody better try to stop him.

The next few minutes passed in silence as all the recipes were tested and evaluated. All of the cookies had turned out well. Kelly felt she could never have decided which one was best, but she did quickly choose a favorite—Emily's Seven-Layer Squares. They were deceivingly simple for the incredible taste they had. She was sure they would be Greg's favorite as well. His box would contain an abundance of these. The cookie boxes were the girls' surprise for the boys. They had not mentioned their night of baking to Greg and Brent.

It was almost midnight by the time the last pan had been pulled from the oven, and all of the cookies had been cooled, wrapped, and either boxed or stored for family consumption. There were twenty-five boxes going to friends and neighbors, and a large assortment of cookies going home with Julie.

It took no encouragement from Peggy for the girls to stumble upstairs and collapse on the bed. They quickly changed and crawled under the comforter. With none of their usual chatter, they were soon asleep.

SIX

Brent was the first one up on Saturday morning. Reaching over, he gave Greg's shoulder a firm shake before he disappeared into the bathroom. Minutes later Greg could hear the shower start. Rolling over, he groaned when he saw the clock. Seven? They hadn't gotten to bed until one the night before. Why in the world did he have to be in Washington with a morning person? he wondered. Washington. He was in Washington, D.C.! As awareness of his surroundings flooded his sleepy mind, Greg threw back the covers and tossed his pillow at the still sleeping Mr. Jackson. He didn't want to miss a single minute of this day. His experience of the city at night had only whetted his appetite for exploring it more fully in daylight.

They were on the streets by eight. Already the city was alive and bustling. A short walk put them in front of the Chesapeake Bagel Bakery on Connecticut Avenue. As the door swung open, Greg took deep breaths of the incredible aroma pouring out onto the streets. He smiled in anticipation.

Brent noticed. "Get ready for a treat," he said. "They make all their own bagels from scratch here. My favorite are the cinnamon raisin and the whole wheat. And there's plenty of cream cheese and homemade preserves."

Less than an hour later the three emerged, full and happy.

"It's a good thing we're walking everywhere this weekend," Mr. Jackson commented, "or we might all gain about ten pounds. Trying to keep up with you guys in the eating category is quite a feat."

Brent grinned at his father. "We're still young, Dad. We can use the excuse of being growing boys."

"Yeah, well I can use the excuse of trying to maintain an energy level high enough to compete with you two!" He laughed. "Besides, this isn't a weekend for self-discipline. It's a weekend for fun and overindulgence."

The three headed once more toward the mall area. Of all the museums Greg wanted to see, the National Air and Space Museum and the Museum of American History were tops on his list. The entire morning was taken up with meandering through just these two buildings.

Greg's favorite part of the Museum of American History was the Foucault Pendulum. Stopping next to the impressive exhibit, he looked up to where the heavy pendulum hung suspended high from the ceiling and then read the sign stationed beside the railing: "You are invited to witness the earth revolve."

Brent's father grinned at his look of skepticism. "Hard to believe, huh?"

"What does it mean?" Greg asked.

"Well, the pendulum never quits swinging from side to side. See all of those red cones on the floor that form a circle around it?"

Greg nodded.

"If we stayed here long enough, we would see all of those red cones knocked over one by one. Since the pendulum never varies its arc, the only way for that to happen is for the earth to revolve beneath it."

"Neat!" Greg stood entranced for a few minutes before Brent convinced him to keep going.

Next they visited the Air and Space Museum. Greg was sure he could have spent the entire day in just that one museum. From the size of the crowds inside, there were *a lot* of people who felt that way.

"This museum is a favorite," Brent's father continued his educational monologue. "It averages about nine million visitors a year. Y'all roam around for a few minutes. I'm going to get us tickets to the film in Langley Theater. We can explore for a couple of hours and then right before lunch there is a showing of the movie *To Fly*. It's magnificent. I just hope you don't get motion sickness. You may never get another chance to actually feel like you're a pilot."

Brent nodded enthusiastically. "The theater is neat. The screen is five stories high and seven stories wide. You actually feel like you're in the middle of the action. I've wanted to see this film for a while."

The morning flew by as they went from one fascinating exhibit to the other. At one point Greg turned to Brent, "We have to bring the girls up here. Kelly and Julie would love this. And it would really be fun to explore together."

When they could no longer ignore their growling stomachs, they headed down the mall area past the towering Capitol building to Union Station.

"Wow!" Greg realized he was using this one little word quite a lot, but it expressed his feelings well. Head back, he gazed upward at what Brent had told him was a ninety-six foot barrel-vault ceiling. It was ringed by a balcony adorned with sculptures of Roman legionnaires. There seemed to be acres of marble flooring reflecting the multitude of Christmas lights and decorations that brought the place to life. But it was all the action that mesmerized Greg. People were everywhere—shopping, eating in one of the many cafes and restaurants, or just strolling around. Groups of singers and bands played an assortment of yuletide music. There was definitely nothing like this in Kingsport.

Brent's father let the two boys soak it in, and then headed down the main hall. "Let's go get something to eat. If I don't have some food, I'm going to starve right here!"

A few minutes later they were seated in the American Restaurant. They had been lucky enough to get a balcony seat overlooking the Main Hall so they could see all the action. After giving their order, Mr. Jackson offered some interesting information about Union Station.

"When this place opened in 1907, it was the largest train station in the world. It took four years to build. In its heyday it was its own mini-city. There was a bowling alley, a mortuary, a YMCA hotel, a hospital, and many other enterprises. When the railroad business began to decline, the station fell on hard times. When the entire building was sealed in 1981, parts of the roof were caving in, floors were buckling up, and the rats of Washington had made it their home. That same year Congress decided to allocate funds to restore it. It took seven years of work and $180,000,000 to turn it into what you see now. It's only been open a few years, but it's realized all the hopes people had for it. This is definitely a happening place. I never miss coming here."

"It's one of my favorite places, too," Brent added. "Being here at Christmas is great. There's always *something* happening, but this is incredible!"

Greg enjoyed the thick burger placed before him, but his attention was riveted on all that was happening below him. He was sure he would never grow tired of this place. Now that he had been here once, he knew he would be back many more times. He wondered if he would ever discover all this city had to offer.

• • •

Kelly could barely bring herself to move when the alarm went off at seven Saturday morning. She managed to sneak an arm out to silence it, but the rest of her remained in a prone position. Dimly she heard the phone ring.

Minutes later, Peggy, still in her pajamas and obviously just awake herself, appeared at her door. "Good news, Kelly. That was Granddaddy Porter. The rain is still coming down, and the forecast says it's going to continue the rest of the day. He's canceled classes."

That's all Kelly needed to hear. Lifting her head from the pillow, she flashed Peggy a thankful grin, rolled over, and went back to sleep. It was ten before she opened her eyes again. Julie awoke at the same time. After mumbled good mornings, they contented themselves with gazing out the window at the rain. Rumbling stomachs and the smell of bacon wafting up the stairs finally convinced them to get up. Minutes later, clad in thick sweats, they ran downstairs to the warmth of the kitchen where Peggy and Emily were eating the traditional Saturday morning breakfast of pancakes and bacon.

Kelly poured the batter and flipped while Julie fixed their drinks and set out two more plates. Within a few minutes they were seated at the table.

"Rain isn't really one of my favorite things, but you looked like an angel this morning when you told me I didn't have to get up because Granddaddy had called off classes," Kelly said to Peggy. "I can't even think of the last time I got to sleep until ten in the morning." Heaving a deep sigh, she gazed out the window. "Rain, glorious rain."

Peggy laughed. "I'm afraid your father isn't sharing your sentiments. He has to show three houses this morning. I finally had to drop an ice cube on his back to get him up. And then, boy, did he get up. I'm surprised you didn't hear us!"

Kelly and Julie both laughed and dug into their steaming pancakes.

Emily finished off her glass of milk and turned to Peggy. "I told Shannon you would pick her up at eleven-thirty to go to the mall. Is that still okay?"

"That's fine."

"Julie and I were wanting to go to the mall today, too," Kelly said. "Could you drop us off at the same time? Julie's mom said she would pick us up this afternoon and drop me off here at the house."

Peggy nodded as she collected dishes from the table. "I'll be happy to. We'll need to leave here in thirty minutes if we're going to be at Shannon's on time."

Kelly and Julie finished gulping down their breakfast, put their dishes in the dishwasher, and headed for the shower. Thirty minutes later, clad in blue jeans and thick sweaters, they dashed through rain to the waiting car.

• • •

"I knew the mall would be crowded today, but this is a madhouse!"

Kelly nodded in agreement with Julie's words. "Everybody in Kingsport must be here. Not only are there people Christmas shopping, I think everyone decided this is the perfect way to spend a rainy day. I feel like a cow in a herd!"

"Let's go over to the Food Court and come up with a plan of action." Julie suggested. "That's better than being mindlessly pulled along by the flow."

Kelly allowed Julie to lead the way as they dodged and weaved their way through the throngs of people. They were lucky enough to walk by a table just as it was being vacated. Kelly dropped down into a chair while Julie went to stand in line to get them drinks. While Kelly waited, she looked around. Stationed outside of the Food Court was a colored fountain surrounded by gaily lit Christmas trees. Wicker reindeer and sleighs were poised on top of an artificial layer of snow. As she watched, a line of men and women filed onto the elevated platform hidden by the snow scene. Minutes later their voices competed with the crowds as they sang a medley of Christmas carols. Kelly cupped her chin in her hands and listened.

"They're good, aren't they?" Julie sat her drink down in front of her.

"Yeah. I don't think I'll ever get tired of Christmas music. We start playing it in our house the first day of December, and I always hate to put it away."

"You really like Christmas, don't you?"

"Sure. Don't you?"

Julie hesitated and searched for words. "I like what Christmas is supposed to be, but I'm not sure I like what it's become. Everything is so commercialized. I mean, look around. Christmas is supposed to be a celebration of the birth of Christ. What do you see? Christmas trees, carolers, reindeers, flowers, and lots of lights. Where's Christ in all this?"

"I know what you mean," Kelly nodded thoughtfully. "I think this Christmas means more to me than any other, though. This will be the first year that I've known Christ personally. For the first time I feel like I know what I'm celebrating. It used to just be a lot of fun and a time to get great presents. But I think maybe you can have both."

"What do you mean?"

"Well, I know there are a lot of people who don't know the meaning of Christmas, so it's just a lot of commercialism and a fun holiday. But so much of what we do for Christmas is what makes it special. I think it's okay to love Christmas trees and lights. I think it's okay to want to show people love by giving them things. I think it's okay to decorate your home and have parties—as long as you don't lose the focus for why it's happening. I think as long as you put Christ in the center of everything, he'll balance it out."

Julie regarded her friend closely. "It seems like you've thought about this a lot."

"I guess I have. Greg and I have talked about it some. So have Peggy and I. I think I was afraid to really enjoy Christmas the same this year, but now I've realized that I'm going to enjoy it even more!" Suddenly she put down her drink and stared at her friend.

"What?" Julie exclaimed. "Are you okay?"

"I just had a great idea. Why don't we have a birthday party for Jesus?" Julie's expression invited her to continue. "Nobody usually has anything to do on Christmas night. All the presents are open and dinner has been eaten. We could have it at my house. It could be simple. Just a time to say happy birthday to Jesus on his day. What do you think?"

Julie nodded with excitement. "I think it's a great idea. It always seemed silly to me that we celebrated his birthday by doing everything for other people. I know I would want some attention on *my* birthday. Let's do it."

Sipping their drinks they made plans for the party. Once that was taken care of, they talked through what they wanted to buy for whom, how much money they had, and what stores they wanted to go to. It seemed like every few minutes they were hailed by one friend or another.

"See. I told you the whole town of Kingsport was here!" Kelly exclaimed. "I think I've seen or talked to everyone I know in this town."

Julie nodded and finished off her drink. "We might as well enter the herd. It's not going to get any better."

Four hours later they stumbled back to the Food Court and again were lucky enough to snag an empty table. This time Julie kept watch over the packages while Kelly went to purchase tacos and drinks.

"Let's get our pictures taken with Santa!"

Julie looked up in confusion as Kelly dumped the tacos in front of her. "Huh?"

Kelly's blue eyes were dancing. "I saw Stacey and Blair getting their pictures taken while I was standing in line. I think the boys would love them."

"But with Santa Claus? Talk about the epitome of commercialism!"

"Oh, come on, Julie. It's not like we're paying homage to him. It's just a picture. It'll be fun."

"Oh, okay. I guess you're right. The boys will probably love them."

They only had to wait in line for thirty minutes before their turn came. Kelly could not stop laughing as the little elf took her picture with the bearded, jolly man whose lap she was sitting on. Julie was right behind her. Ten minutes later they had their coveted pictures. Both were pleased with the results.

"I'll give my mom a call to pick us up," Julie said. "It should only take her about ten minutes to get

here. I'll tell her to meet us at the entrance where
the movie theaters are."

"Okay. I'll hold the packages while you call."

Five minutes later they were standing just inside
the door, watching the flow of cars for Julie's mom.

"I wonder if Greg and Brent are having a good
time," Kelly mused.

Julie turned serious. "I sure hope so. Brent
doesn't talk much about his family, but I think he
was really looking forward to this trip with his dad. I
hope it's going well."

• • •

"You can have the shower first, Greg."

Greg groaned and fell across the bed. "Thanks,
but no thanks. My body refuses to do one more
thing. I want to just lay here and let my feet thank
me for finally giving them a break. You go ahead. I'll
be ready to stand up again when you get out."

Brent grinned, grabbed some clothes, and disappeared into the bathroom.

"I'm glad to see you looking as tired as I am."
Brent's father walked through the door and collapsed on the opposite bed. "It makes me feel not so
old." Yawning, he stretched out. "Wake me after
you take a shower. Even a thirty-minute nap will
revive me. I just made reservations at a really special
restaurant for tonight. It's six now. Our reservations
are for seven-thirty, so we need to leave here by
seven-fifteen. I think you guys will like it."

Greg smiled and nodded. He was sure he would.

Thirty minutes later when he emerged from the
bathroom, Greg could feel the tension in the room.

Brent was sitting stiffly on the bed; his father was running his hand through his hair in frustration. Greg hesitated, not sure what to do. Mr. Jackson noticed him and forced a smile.

"Looks like it's my turn in the shower. It won't take me long." Grabbing his clothes, he paused at the bathroom door. "We're going to be having company tonight, Greg. My fiancé is in town on business. She will be joining us." With those words he turned and disappeared into the bathroom.

Brent remained where he was on the bed and said nothing. Greg was uncertain of what he should do. Would it be better to try and get Brent to talk or to just not say anything? Certain his friend wouldn't open up with his dad so close, Greg opted to turn on the television and offer Brent a diversion while they finished getting ready.

Fifteen minutes later when Brent's father reappeared, Greg tried to ease the situation by talking about what they had done that afternoon. He knew he was rambling but talking about their time in the Capitol building and the Senate Chambers filled in the tense quiet. When the clock said it was time to go, he grabbed his coat, glad to be escaping what had become a confining room.

Mr. Jackson's next words made the situation worse. "I know you're not happy with Allison being here tonight, Brent, but I hope you'll make the best of it. It might be better if you don't mention her being here to your mother. There is no reason to upset her."

Greg watched Brent's eyes flash as his mouth tightened, but his friend merely gave a curt nod, reached for his coat, and headed for the elevator. Greg followed close behind. This promised to be an interesting evening.

The Iron Gate Inn was enough to take Greg's mind off the tense situation for a little while. Their short walk from the hotel had led them to a converted stable. Greg discovered that their seating was a booth inside of an old horse stall. A big fire was blazing in the immense brick fireplace. The smells coming from the kitchen made his mouth start watering as soon as they sat down. Glancing outside, he took note of the grape arbor and magnolia tree that graced the brick walled garden set in the back. On the way over, Mr. Jackson had told him that the owners, the Saah family, had once supervised the kitchens for the king of Arabia. The menu consisted of delicious middle eastern food. Greg knew he was going to add another item to his list of new experiences.

They had just been seated when an attractive woman paused at the hostess desk and then headed in their direction. Greg could feel Brent's tension increase.

"Allison! I'm so glad you could join us." Rising, Brent's father allowed her to slip into the booth and then slid in beside her.

"Hello, Eric. Hello, Brent."

"Hello, Allison." Brent made no attempt to hide the hardness in his voice.

Brent's father spoke quickly in an attempt to ease the situation. "Allison, this is Greg, a friend of Brent's from Kingsport."

She smiled pleasantly. "Hello, Greg. It's nice to meet you."

"It's nice to meet you, too." Greg was determined to do all he could to make the night easier for his friend.

Throughout the rest of the evening, Greg tried to cover for his friend's morose silence. If Brent was addressed directly, he would give terse yes or no answers, but he refused to be drawn into the conversation. Greg could tell Mr. Jackson was becoming more and more irritated. The food was delicious, but Greg couldn't say he really enjoyed it. The whole affair was very tense. He was quite glad when the check had been paid and they rose to leave.

Brent and Greg waited beside the door as his father walked Allison to her car. He returned shortly and without a word turned toward the hotel. The short walk was accomplished in silence. As they moved into the lobby, Mr. Jackson turned to the two boys.

"I'll be back later. Don't bother to wait up for me." With those words he turned and disappeared into the night.

Brent stared after him.

S E V E N

As Brent continued to stare at the door his father had disappeared through, Greg searched for words to say. None came. As Greg watched, he could sense his friend struggling with his feelings. Maybe this would be enough to make him talk about what was going on.

Forcing a grin to his face, Brent turned and gave a short laugh. "Looks like we're on our own. Want to go for a swim?"

Greg was caught off guard. How in the world could Brent switch his feelings so fast? Where had he learned to so completely cover his emotions? Greg had been sure Brent was ready to blow, but he seemed to be once more in control of the situation.

"A swim?"

"Yeah." Brent nodded. "It's not even ten. The health club stays open until midnight. We have time to go for a swim and then use the jacuzzi. It would be a great way to relax our muscles after all the walking and stuff we did today."

"You sure you want to do that?"

"Why wouldn't I? We said we were going to make the most of our time here, didn't we? Let's do it."

Greg's mind raced. Should he let Brent keep running from his situation? "Do you want to talk about tonight?"

Brent's laugh was more forced this time. "There's nothing to talk about. I should be used to it by now." Turning, he headed toward the elevator. It was clear he didn't intend to say anything more.

Sighing, Greg followed him. *Lord,* Greg prayed, *when it's your time, you're going to have to tear down his walls and get him to talk. I don't know how to make him.*

They stayed in their room only long enough to pick up their trunks and some towels. Then they headed down the long corridor to the health club and swimming pool. Once again, Greg found himself in the lap of luxury. Warm water lapped against the sides of the Olympic-size swimming pool. Dimly lit lanterns hanging under the massive skylight arching over the pool offered the only light. Tall trees and an abundance of plants gave the appearance of a tropical setting. There was even music playing softly. Ten-fifteen on a Saturday night must not have been a popular time for pool use. They were the only ones there.

Greg and Brent changed, lined up on the sides of the pool, and then cut the water cleanly with their long dives. Back and forth they swam, releasing all the tension from their miles of walking that day. When Greg had had enough, he floated lazily on his back. Brent continued to stroke up and down the pool. Greg sensed he was trying to release all his pent-up emotions. He supposed it was better than blowing up.

Greg was so relaxed he wasn't even aware when Brent quit swimming and moved over to join him.

"How about hitting the jacuzzi?" Brent asked. "I found the switch to turn on the jets."

Greg's response was to swim over and haul himself from the pool. "It doesn't take any persuasion to get me in a jacuzzi. My muscles are saying thank you before I even get there."

Brent hit a switch, and the steaming water became a bubbling cauldron. Both boys sighed as they lowered their bodies into its inviting depths. Greg grinned at Brent, closed his eyes, and allowed every part of himself to relax.

Thirty minutes later, Greg hauled himself from the water, uncertain his relaxed body would be able to carry him back to the room. Collapsing on the chaise lounge next to the jacuzzi, he stared up at the skylight.

Brent dropped down next to him. "I wouldn't mind having one of those at home. What a great way to end every day."

Greg nodded. "You got that right. I bet you'd never have trouble sleeping if you had a jacuzzi. I'd want it close to my bedroom, though. Right now our room seems a hundred miles away. We're going to have to lay here for a few minutes before I can walk back."

"No problem. Dad won't mind if we're late getting in. I left him a note to let him know where we were going. I was kinda thinking he would come join us."

Greg thought otherwise. Mr. Jackson had been pretty mad when he left them in the lobby. Had he been going to meet Allison?

Emptiness greeted them when they entered their hotel room twenty minutes later. Greg could tell Brent was disappointed. His friend looked around as if he couldn't believe his father wasn't there.

Now's the time to get him to talk. Greg recognized the still, small voice of God. "Your father's still gone."

"Yeah." Brent's voice registered his pain and disbelief.

"What's going on in your family, Brent?"

As usual, Brent tried to evade Greg's questions. "What do you mean? It's nothing. Dad must be doing something."

Greg knew he was going to have to push. "It's not nothing, Brent. Something is eating at you. You don't ever talk about what's happening in your family. You were miserable at dinner tonight. You may think you're doing a good job of hiding your feelings, but you're not."

Brent wheeled around from where he was standing beside the bed and shouted, "So what do you want to know? Do you want to hear all the gory details about how my dad left my mom for Allison? Do you want to hear how I've been in the middle of their mess for the last year and a half? Do you want to hear me say how much I hate them for what they're doing to me? Will that make you happy?"

"We're friends, Brent." Greg struggled for the right words. "Everyone needs someone to talk to. I just want to help."

Brent stared hard at his friend and then collapsed onto the bed. "Yeah. Okay. I'm sorry I yelled at you. I'm just a little uptight right now."

Greg waited quietly for Brent to continue.

"Dad started seeing Allison a year and a half ago." Every word seemed painful for Brent. "I saw them together one night and figured out what was going on. When I confronted Dad with it, he talked me into keeping it a secret. I agreed because I didn't want Mom to be hurt. I mean, heck, he's my dad. I wanted to make him happy. I guess I thought maybe it would blow over, too. But I hated lying to Mom. I knew she was beginning to be suspicious."

Taking a deep breath, Brent went on, "Six months after that Dad walked out on us. He said he didn't love Mom and that he never would again. He was in love with Allison and wanted to marry her. Mom was crushed. She cried almost all the time for two weeks. When she quit crying, she became really bitter. I can't say I blame her. Dad really shafted us. He's got plenty of money, and he has to give Mom a certain amount every month until the divorce settlement is all taken care of. But he makes her ask for it every time. She hates to do it, so she makes me do it. I hate it, too, but I know she needs my help right now. Dad likes to make her feel bad by giving me expensive stuff."

"Like this trip." Greg remembered Brent's earlier tenseness about the restaurant.

"Yeah. Dad is blowing a wad on this one. And Mom is always talking bad about Dad. I know what he's doing is wrong, but he's my dad and I still love him—even though I hate him most of the time now ...." Brent's voice trailed off in confusion. "Dad doesn't say many bad things about Mom. He mostly just chooses to ignore the fact that they were married for eighteen years. All he talks about is how wonderful Allison is. Every time we go somewhere at home, he wants her to be with us. He seems convinced that I will love and accept her if he keeps pushing her down my throat. All it's doing is making it worse. And then he always reminds me that Mom doesn't need to know Allison was there. He just wants me to keep lying for him. I guess he figures the divorce settlement will go better. It's stupid. I always feel like I'm stuck in the middle, trying to keep the peace. In the meantime, it's driving me crazy! I hoped this weekend would be better. I mean we're in Washington, D.C.—four hours from home! I thought it would just be the three of us. I should have known Allison would show up. I just didn't think it would happen . . ."

As Brent grew quiet, the door to the room opened. Greg almost groaned out loud. Brent had just spilled his guts, and Greg wasn't going to be able to respond. Greg hoped that Brent's father would say something to make his son feel better. It didn't take long to realize that wasn't going to happen.

Mr. Jackson breezed in as if nothing had happened. Walking into the bathroom he noticed the wet suits hanging on the shower rod. Smiling at Greg, he spoke to him, "Did you guys have a good swim? I was hoping you would get over there while we were here."

Greg nodded. "It was fun."

"Good." Glancing at Brent, he still didn't say anything to him. "I know there are some things you guys want to squeeze in in the morning. Guess we'd better get some sleep." Disappearing into the bathroom, they could hear him whistling softly as he got ready for bed.

As Greg watched, he saw a depth of hopelessness come into Brent's eyes that he hadn't seen before. A curtain seemed to close over his heart. All emotion fled from his face.

Standing, Brent peeled off his clothes, put on shorts and a T-shirt, and crawled into bed. Reaching up, he flicked off the light over the bed and turned his face to the wall.

Greg felt helpless. He could feel the depression settling over his friend, and he had no idea how to stop it.

EIGHT

I'll be by to pick you up for the Christmas party at six." Greg said to Brent as Mr. Jackson drove up to his house. "That gives us about an hour to take showers and get ready for the girls." Turning to Brent's father, Greg once more thanked him for the weekend. He grabbed his bag and was stepping out of the car when Brent spoke.

"I don't think I'll be going to the party tonight."

Greg turned back. "Huh?"

"I'm not feeling too well." Brent forced a short laugh. "I guess all our activity this weekend wore me out. And I've got a big chemistry test tomorrow. I've studied for it, but I don't want to be exhausted when I take it. Tell Julie I'm sorry. I'll see her at school tomorrow."

There was plenty Greg wanted to say, but he couldn't with Brent's father there. He knew his friend wasn't sick, but he couldn't *make* him go to the party. So he just nodded his head. "Yeah. I'll tell her. Hey, I hope you feel better. Maybe a good night's sleep will help."

Brent's nod was listless, and he didn't bother to respond. He simply shifted his position in the front seat and stared out the window.

• • •

Kelly gave Greg a big hug after she ran down the stairs to meet him in the kitchen. "Greetings, Washington boy! How was the weekend?"

Scott and Peggy walked in from the den. "Greg!" Peggy smiled. "How was your weekend? It was weird not having you around to beg for food."

"My weekend was great! And speaking of begging..." Greg cast his eyes toward the plate of cookies perched on the counter.

Kelly laughed, reached for the plate, and handed it to him.

With a mouth full of sugar cookies, Greg gave them a brief description of his activities since he and Kelly had said goodbye two days before. Kelly knew she would get the full story that night.

Her father shook his head and laughed. "You make me tired just listening to you. I'm surprised you're still moving."

Greg grinned. "I'm pretty tired, but I had so much fun it was worth it. I can hardly wait to go back. There's still so much I want to see. I feel like I just barely scratched the surface."

"Maybe, but it sounds like you gave it the deepest scratch you could manage," Peggy teased.

"You bet I did." Grabbing a couple of more cookies, Greg took Kelly's hand in his empty one. "Time to go, my girl. Julie is waiting for us. Have you got enough clothes on to stay warm?"

"I would certainly hope so. Two layers on the bottom and three on the top. Not to mention my dad's ski coat. I think this should do the job."

They said goodbye and headed for the car. Kelly jumped in and then turned to Greg as he slipped behind the wheel. "Where's Brent? You usually pick him up on the way over."

Greg's face clouded over with the concern he felt for his friend. In the ten minutes it took to get to Julie's house, he filled Kelly in on the events of the weekend. "I'm really concerned about Brent, Kelly. He looked kind of dead when he dropped me off. Like he was hopeless or something. I don't know what to do. I was so glad when he opened up last night, but we haven't had a minute alone to talk since then. The funny thing is, I don't think he wants to. We could have been alone today, but he made sure his father was always around. It's like he's scared to have me say anything."

Kelly listened, but she didn't know what to say. "He's in a pretty tough place. I guess it's going to take some time to work it out. At least he knows you care."

"Yeah. I hope it's enough."

Greg's words gave Kelly an uneasy feeling in her stomach.

Julie's face clouded with disappointment when she climbed into the car and didn't find Brent, but she seemed to understand. "I'll see him tomorrow. I hope some rest will make him feel better."

Greg doubted rest had anything to do with it, but there was no reason to burden Julie with Brent's depression. Once again he prayed for his friend and then tried to give it to the Lord so he could enjoy the evening with Kelly and Julie.

• • •

Everyone was crowded into the youth room when they heard a rumbling outside. Suddenly the door burst open, and Martin and Janie appeared dressed in country garb.

"Your hayride has arrived!" Martin announced. "Come on out and load up."

The group exchanged mystified looks as they jumped up and headed for the door. Steve, who was in the lead, sounded disappointed as his voice drifted back to where Greg, Kelly, and Julie were waiting to get out.

"Oh man, it's just the bus. What's this deal about a hayride?" Seconds later they heard his loud laugh and whoop of excitement. "Look at this! Now *this* is the way to have a hayride!"

Moments later they clambered on the bus and joined in everyone's excitement. Martin had indeed transformed the bus into a hay wagon. With the help of several parents he had taken all the seats out of the bus, driven it out to Porter's, and filled it with massive amounts of sweet-smelling hay. The mounds stopped just short of the windows. Scattered around were large containers of popcorn, hot chocolate, and steaming cider. Christmas music was blaring forth from a boom box near the front.

Kelly grinned in delight. "This is perfect!" Turning, she gave Martin and Janie big hugs. "You guys are too much. This must have taken hours of work."

"Let's just say we had plenty of good help." Martin climbed behind the wheel and started the engine. "Y'all will want to keep the windows open. The dust could get pretty bad in here if you close it up." Turning to Greg, he requested, "Could you start us off with prayer, Greg? We're going to have a lot of fun tonight, but I'd like to ask God to help us be a blessing to the people we sing for."

"Sure." The group bowed their heads while Greg led them in a brief prayer.

Singing had already started when the bus pulled out of the parking lot. Laughter rang through the air as everyone found their own little niche in the hay and settled in. There was an unspoken agreement that the anticipated hay fight would wait until the way home. They didn't want to go into the nursing home with hair and clothes full of grass.

The next hour and a half flew by. Two neighborhoods were chosen by Julie being blindfolded and pointing at places on the map. That way no one could complain if their area of town wasn't visited. They also stopped in at the hospital and the town nursing home.

Kelly and Greg enjoyed the nursing home the most. Usually it depressed Kelly to go there, but this time the place had almost a festive air. The residents were all waiting for them when they arrived and seemed to really enjoy their singing. Several sang along with them. One old man even played the piano for accompaniment. Kelly was reluctant to leave. She hugged many necks on her way out.

"Why do we only do that at Christmas time?" Kelly asked aloud. "I bet they would enjoy having us come and sing other times of the year, too."

"You're right. It just seems like people always want to do something for people at Christmas. Spreading it out over the year would make a lot more sense. It would be fun to plan some other times to come and sing with them." Julie's eyes were shining. The wheels were turning in her head.

"Okay, guys. We're going to take a brief spin out in the country and then we're headed back for the church." Martin started the bus and headed down the road.

Kelly, Greg, and Julie settled down in the hay with Steve, Carrie, and Joe. Greg carried the conversation with descriptions of his weekend in the nation's capital. Kelly had been there before, but she'd been much younger and there had been a large group of them from school. She would love to experience it the way Greg had—at night and then just two or three people roaming during the day. The time passed quickly. Soon they were pulling into the church parking lot.

"We're here. Unload."

Martin's words were the signal everyone had been waiting for. Several people reached over to close lids on the drinks and popcorn, and then war broke out! Hay flew everywhere as great handfuls were grabbed up and heaved. Kelly and Julie were laughing so hard they could hardly bend over to pick it up. Kelly shrieked as Greg grabbed her sweater and stuffed a huge wad down her back. Grabbing his leg, she caught him off balance and sent him sprawling in the hay on his back. Laughing, she scooped up big armfuls and tried to cover him. Lunging forward, he wrapped his arms around her knees and dropped

her on her back. The fighting and playing continued until Martin, laughing, turned out the lights on
the bus and honked the horn.

"Okay, wild people. That's enough. I think you
have very successfully rearranged all the hay in the
bus now—not to mention what's escaped through
the windows and is scattered all over the ground. I'd
say it's time to attack the presents underneath the
tree in the youth room."

Everybody was laughing as they clambered off
the bus and spent the next few minutes de-haying
their bodies. Martin walked out with a few rakes.
Greg joined Steve and Joe in raking around the bus
and piling it back on. Martin would be taking the
bus out to Porter's in the morning and unloading
the hay into one of the hay troughs. The horses
would still eat it, so there was no reason to let it go to
waste. Once their job was finished, they entered the
youth room where everyone was waiting for them.

The only other lights beside the gaily lit Christmas tree were candles that had been set around the
room, giving the place a festive atmosphere. The
next hour of gift exchanging passed in hilarity.
Everyone drew a number to determine their time to
choose a gift. Once their number was called they
could either choose a gift from under the tree or
take an already opened gift away from its owner. An
opened gift could only be reclaimed twice, however,
before the owner could claim permanent rights. If
the number bearer chose an opened gift, then the
person they took it from could choose any gift under
the tree. The most coveted gift was a pair of red
boxers with green Christmas trees.

Kelly had hoped for those, but they had only exchanged hands once when she became their owner. Once she had claimed them, she stuck them under her leg hoping that "out of sight" would be "out of mind." She had no such luck. Steve had kept a close eye on her. He was the last person to select, and he walked directly to where she was sitting and held out his hand.

"Hand them over, Kelly."

She tried to look innocent. "Hand what over, Steve?"

"Good try. I want the boxers you're trying to hide. Let's have them."

Kelly stuck out her tongue and made a face but dutifully handed them over as the rest of the group laughed. Resignedly, she reached for the last package. What she found in the small box delighted her. Folded several times in order to fit in the box was a gift certificate to the local Christian bookstore. Kelly already knew the tape she would buy.

Janie grabbed up the last of the wrapping paper and stuffed it in the huge plastic bag she was hauling around. Martin moved to the front of the room and waited for the chatter and rustling to settle down. When all was quiet he said, "I've asked a couple of you to share your favorite Christmas memories with us. Stephanie, would you come on up?"

Martin sat back down as the cute, red-headed sophomore made her way to the front. Friendly and outgoing, she didn't appear to be nervous at all. Kelly envied her composure.

"Christmas is my favorite time of the year, so it took me a while to come up with my favorite

Christmas." Stephanie began with a big smile. "I finally decided it was the one the year my dad lost his job. Three years ago he got laid off in September and didn't find another job until March. Things were really tight around our house. We usually make a big deal out of Christmas, but we couldn't that year—at least not as far as money was concerned. My two brothers and I were pretty bummed because we thought it wouldn't be any fun. We were sure wrong.

"Dad talked to a friend of his who owns a big farm in the country. Usually we have a huge balsam tree, but that year we drove out and tramped around his farm until we found a cedar we liked. It was prickly and definitely wasn't a balsam, but we had found it and cut it ourselves. I loved it. By the time we got it home and put lights on it, it was beautiful. We even made popcorn chains to put on it because so many of our normal decorations just didn't look right on a cedar.

"We couldn't do any baking that year, but our neighbors and friends knew about our situation and kept the house full of cookies and bread and stuff. We also found everything in town to do that was free. I was amazed how many fun things there are to do that don't cost anything. And since we didn't have money to spend, we gave the gift of ourselves. All of us made coupons—for one another and for neighbors and friends. I gave back rubs, bed-making services, house-cleaning days, yard raking— all kinds of stuff. People loved those gifts. What started out as a horrible Christmas became the best ever. I learned to focus not on getting, but on giving."

Julie and Kelly exchanged glances and grins as Stephanie returned to her seat amid applause. Here was someone they were sure would come to their Happy Birthday, Jesus party. She had the right idea!

"Thanks, Stephanie. Matt? Will you come on up?"

Greg moved over to allow the burly senior to respond to Martin's request. Matt looked like the linebacker he was. For the last three years he had been all-county. Greg sat next to him in chemistry and knew what a great guy he was.

"I'm like Stephanie," Matt said. "It took me a while to figure out what my favorite Christmas was. But not because my family makes a big deal out of them or because there have been so many great ones. Up until two years ago, I hated Christmas."

Greg and Kelly looked at each other in surprise. They didn't know much about Matt other than that he was a good football player and a nice guy. What was his story?

Matt continued, "My folks split up when I was six. There had been a couple of separations before, but that's when they made it final. My dad moved about forty-five minutes from here to a farm. My brother and I spent most weekends with him. When Christmas rolled around, my parents thought we should spend it together as a family. So we did. But my brother and I hated it. There was always a lot of tension, and Mom and Dad would compete to see who gave the best presents. If we liked one better than the other, one of them got hurt.

"About five years ago my dad got remarried. That made it even worse. Now we had to go *both* places on

Christmas day. We would have a big lunch at home after opening presents, and then my dad would pick us up for a big dinner and gifts at his house. You might think having two big meals on Christmas would be great, but it's not. We always had to eat tons to make my mom happy, and then we would have to do the same thing at my dad's. Usually I was still full when I had to do it all over again. And then Dad would ask what Mom got for us, and Mom would want to see everything Dad gave us. The whole thing was a pain. I dreaded Christmas every year because it was such a hassle."

The room was silent as Matt paused. "Two years ago I gave my life to Jesus at a summer camp," he continued. "My whole life started to change. Last year things started to really come together. I finally understood what it meant to make Christ the Lord of my life. I learned to bring things to him and not carry the burden all by myself. When Christmas rolled around last year, the circumstances were the same but I handled them differently. I came to the candlelight Christmas Eve service here at church so my focus would be on Christ. The next morning I got up and had a good quiet time before we were supposed to be downstairs. There were still hard parts of the day, but I prayed through them. That night was what made it so special, though. I had called four of my friends from here at church, and we got together at one of their houses. We sang songs, prayed together, and thanked Jesus for coming as a gift for us. It changed the whole way I looked at Christmas when I realized it's a day to celebrate the greatest gift of all time. It took the focus off myself."

Kelly and Julie exchanged delighted looks for a second time. The list for their party was growing.

Greg listened intently, wishing Brent could be here. He was sure that Matt's sharing would have hit home with him. Once more his mind turned to his friend. What was he feeling? What was he thinking about as he sat at home? Was he okay?

Martin moved to the front of the room as Matt sat down. "Thanks, Matt. Without knowing it, you gave the perfect lead-in for what we're going to do next. Several of you have asked about the manger here in the front of the room. Matt's right when he says the purpose of Christmas is to celebrate the birth of Christ. How would you like it if you had a birthday party and all your guests brought presents for each other, but no one brought anything for you? I don't think I would feel very loved."

He paused long enough to let his words sink in. "I want us to take some time tonight to think about what we can give Jesus as a birthday present. It might be something nice you can do for someone in your family. It might be offering to help a friend. But I can tell you this. What means the most to Jesus is when we give him something of ourselves. Maybe you're holding on to a behavior you know you need to give up. Maybe you have a bad attitude. Maybe you'd like to promise him some time with you every day. We're going to sit quietly for a while and let you think. Janie is passing out paper, pens, and envelopes. Once you know what you want to give him, just write it down, stick it in the envelope, and bring it up to the manger."

Martin stopped and thought for a moment. "Oh, and seal the envelope, and put your name and address on it. This is just between you and God. In a month or so I'll mail the envelopes back to you. Then you can decide how well you're doing with your gift to him."

Silence filled the room for quite some time before papers and pens were put to use. One by one, each person in the room filed forward and placed his or her gift in the manger. No one spoke until the last person had gone up. Martin picked up his guitar and led the group in a couple more soft Christmas carols before he prayed and told them good-night.

Greg used the time to continue praying for Brent. He could not erase the burden he had for his friend from his mind.

NINE

Are we really only two and a half days away from freedom?" Kelly asked as she set down her tray next to Greg's. "I only have one more test to go, and then it's smooth sailing. I thought Grimsley was going to kill me with her French test, but I actually think I did pretty good. I guess my extra studying paid off."

"I'm hoping mine does, too." Greg said. "Chemistry was tough, but I feel good about it. I'm beat, though. I was up until two this morning studying. Once I have French behind me, I can relax."

"Yeah. I think I've already started to relax. I only have English left and that's always a piece of cake for me."

Julie made a face at Kelly. "I can't believe you're so relaxed about English. I'm just hoping I don't blow it. Reading all these heavy books is just not my thing. I'd lots rather be doing history."

Kelly groaned. "You are a strange child, Julie. History is worse than a foreign language to me. I like knowing about what's happened but memorizing all those dates is torture. Guess it just goes to show that we all have different talents."

Brent walked up and laid down his tray. Without a word he pulled out a chair and sat down. Greg, Kelly, and Julie exchanged concerned looks. Brent had been quiet and withdrawn all week. They didn't know what to do.

Greg gave him a big smile. "We weren't sure you were going to join us. Did your chemistry test take longer than you thought it would?"

"No." Brent looked down at his tray. Greg thought that was all he was going to say, but Brent continued, "My soccer coach had some questions about the tournament on Saturday."

Greg tried to keep the conversation alive. "So how did chemistry go? Did you ace it?" He knew science was one of Brent's best subjects.

"No. I'm pretty sure I blew it."

"Yeah, right!" Greg laughed at his comment but then stopped, struck by the look of apathy on Brent's face. "Are you serious?"

Brent shrugged and took a bite of his burger. "It's no big deal. Bad grades aren't the end of the world. English and history are probably going to be the same. This school thing is getting pretty old. It won't matter soon, anyway."

Once again his friends exchanged concerned looks. Brent had always been a really good student. They knew he had big plans for college. What was going on?

Greg had tried to get Brent alone to talk several times since they had gotten back from Washington, but Brent was becoming a master at avoiding him. He had called a couple of times, but Brent always made an excuse to get off the phone. He didn't know what to do. He knew his friend was depressed. He sensed it was getting worse.

Looking up, Brent caught their looks of concern. Laughing, he shook his head at them. "Hey, lighten up, you guys. They were only tests. I had great grades going in to them. It's not the end of the world if I blew them. I'll make up for it." Shaking off his sullen mood, he launched into talk about the weekend's upcoming soccer tournament. "Coach Mullins says he feels really good about our taking the tournament this year. Clinton High is the only one who has a team good enough to beat us, but he thinks we're stronger than they are this year. Wouldn't it be great if we could win the trophy back?"

Knowing they couldn't get Brent to talk if they tried, the three friends allowed him to draw them into casual conversation.

As they talked, Kelly was aware of how confused Julie was by Brent's behavior. Julie cared for Brent, but she had confided the day before that she felt like she was on a roller coaster. She never knew what to expect anymore. One minute, Brent would be his friendly, caring self. The next, he would withdraw and become very distant. The withdrawn, distant moments were occurring more and more often. Julie felt sure she was doing something wrong for his moods to swing so radically. Kelly had tried to assure her that Brent was just dealing with some hard stuff in his family and that it wasn't her fault. She had even shared with her much of what had happened in Washington. But Julie was still convinced she should be able to keep Brent from being so depressed.

Kelly tried to pull Julie into the conversation in order to keep her mind off Brent. "What time do you have to be at school tonight to get ready for your concert?" It was a question Kelly already knew the answer to, but she couldn't think of anything else to say.

Julie's look told her she knew what Kelly was doing, but she obliged her with an answer. "Six."

"My dad is giving me the car for tonight, so I'll pick everyone up," Greg offered. "The concert starts at seven-thirty, but I want to make sure we get good seats. I'm going to pick Kelly up at six-fifteen so that will put me at your house at six-thirty, Brent."

"Okay." Finishing off his sandwich, Brent stood to leave.

Julie looked at her watch in dismay. "We still have fifteen minutes, Brent. Where are you going?"

Brent shrugged and turned away. "I've got some stuff I need to do. I'll see you tonight."

Kelly reached over to squeeze Julie's hand as tears flooded her eyes. Julie shook her head but didn't say anything. Greg thought about following his friend, but he didn't really feel like it would do any good, so he stayed put.

Kelly turned to him. "What are we going to do? Brent seems to be getting worse, not better. I can't believe he blew all those tests. How are we going to help him?"

Greg shook his head in frustration. "I don't know, Kelly. I can't get him to talk to me. I keep hoping he'll just snap out of it. Maybe we just need to give him some more time." His concerned look indicated that he didn't really believe that but didn't know what else to do. "Maybe the break from school will help him."

The concert went well that night, but Brent remained drawn and distant. School would be out in just two days. And they had big plans for Friday night.

• • •

Greg had just hung up the phone from talking with Kelly when Brent called.

"Brent, I just finished talking with Kelly. She says everything is set for tonight. Granddaddy has given us the okay to come out and go hiking, and he told us an area in the woods where there is some wood left over from a campfire some people had this summer. The weather is even cooperating. The clouds are clearing so the full moon will make it like day. I'm leaving in ten minutes. I'll be by your house soon."

"I'm not going to be able to go, Greg."

Greg's heart sank at the apathy he heard in Brent's voice. He and Kelly and Julie had thought keeping him busy would help. Now Brent was backing out on them—again. Keeping his voice casual, Greg asked, "What's the problem?"

"Oh, it's no big deal," Brent replied, "but I'm just not feeling too well. I don't want to get sick before the big tournament tomorrow, so I decided I'd better stay home. The three of you will have a good time without me. Or maybe we could make it tomorrow night. I'm sure I'll be feeling better by then."

Greg seriously doubted that there was anything physically wrong with his friend. Frustration knotted his stomach. "Are you going to call Julie?"

"Do me a favor and take care of that for me, will you? I tried to call a few minutes ago, but her phone was busy. I'd like to go ahead and go to bed."

Once again Greg doubted Brent was telling the truth. He felt a surge of anger over Brent's attitude. Didn't he know what he was doing to Julie? Didn't he care that all of them were concerned about him? Didn't their friendship mean anything to him? But Greg didn't say anything. He knew his answer was short. "Yeah, I'll take care of it. Hope you feel better. See you tomorrow."

Greg called Julie and explained the situation to her. Then he added, "Why don't we change it to tomorrow night? The three of us can plan something else to do tonight. What do you think?"

"Look," Julie tried to sound casual, "if Brent's not going, I think I'll let you and Kelly have the evening to yourself. My folks are going to the mall, and I have a few things I could pick up there to finish my Christmas shopping."

Greg's anger toward Brent rose again as he heard the hurt in Julie's voice. "Are you sure?"

"I'm sure," Julie sighed. "I'll see you guys tomorrow at the soccer tournament. I'm planning on getting there at nine. What about you?"

"I'll be there at nine, too. Kelly has lessons tomorrow, but she'll be there by twelve-thirty. The big games won't be till the afternoon anyway."

"Okay. I'll see you then."

Greg shook his head and then called Kelly.

• • •

"I'd say this is a night for bareback riding. Any extra warmth will be greatly appreciated!" Kelly shivered.

Greg nodded as he rubbed his hands together. "This is a beautiful night for riding, but boy it is *cold*. The thermometer says it's only twenty degrees. Some people would say we're crazy."

Kelly laughed. "I think *most* people would say we're crazy. But who cares? Full-moon nights are made for riding. Besides, I have a surprise for you."

"What is it?"

"If I told you, it wouldn't be a surprise, silly."

Greg grinned at her and then gave Shandy a quick brushing before slipping his bridle on. It took Kelly only a few minutes to have Crystal ready as well. They were just finishing when Granddaddy strolled into the barn.

"I didn't really believe y'all would come out here on a night like this. When I saw the light, I had to come prove to myself you were really this crazy. You'll be lucky if you don't freeze to death." Shaking his head, he had only one more thing to say, "Kids!"

Kelly laughed and ran over to give him a hug. "It's going to be great, Granddaddy. And besides, I can remember stories you've told me about riding on full-moon nights in the winter. Where do you think I got the idea?"

A reluctant smile appeared on the old man's weathered face. "Okay. You're right. I'm probably just jealous. Y'all have a good time. You can come over for hot chocolate when you get back, if you want to. I imagine I'll still be up."

"Thanks, Granddaddy." Kelly gave him another gentle squeeze. "The hot chocolate sounds good. We'll probably drop in if it's not too late. I'm sure our bodies will freeze solid before too long."

"I imagine you're right." With an affectionate smile, the old man disappeared into the night.

Thirty minutes later, Kelly rode up to a gate on the far side of the farm and leaned over to open it. She had been working with Crystal on this skill, and her filly was getting much better. Tonight she was perfect. She stood rock still as Kelly swung the gate over, and then she backed to where Kelly could reach down and latch it again.

Greg regarded her curiously as he rode Shandy through the gate. "What gives? What are we doing here? I don't think we've ever been in this field before."

"You're right. You've never been here before." Kelly said nothing more but continued to ride forward.

"I take it this is part of my surprise."

"I think you are a very smart boy," Kelly teased.

Minutes later they rounded a curve in the trail. "There is your surprise."

"Cows?" Greg obviously didn't know how to react.

"Yes, cows."

"I don't get it." He made no attempt to hide his confusion.

Kelly just grinned. Urging Crystal into a canter, she called back over her shoulder, "Just watch me." With those words, she urged Crystal into a gallop as she drove straight into the herd of cattle, yelling Indian cries as she did. She laughed aloud as the cattle scattered in every direction. Having completed her riotous act, she circled back around to where Greg was watching her with a grin. "Now we round them up."

For the next hour they amused themselves by weaving back and forth in order to maneuver the cattle back into a herd. Once they had the cows all in one area, they began their war whoops and sent them scattering again. The full moon illuminated the pasture like day. Their laughter rang in the still air like a choir of silver bells.

After the second time they had the cows herded together, Greg pulled Shandy alongside Crystal. "It's probably better that I don't know, but where did these cows come from?"

"Granddaddy had them brought in a few days ago. He got a really good deal on them, so he's going to winter them over here. All of them are bred. Once they have their calves, he'll sell them all."

"Another question I probably don't want to know the answer to: Does he have any idea we're out here terrorizing his cows?"

"Well . . . not exactly."

"Not exactly?" Greg fixed Kelly with a questioning gaze.

"Well . . . I didn't exactly tell him we were coming out here, but it was one of his stories that gave me the idea," Kelly said defensively. "I didn't figure he would get too mad. Besides," she grinned, "no one could ever possibly know we were out here. I haven't exactly seen anyone else, have you?"

Greg laughed as he shook his head. "Hey, I was just asking. I'm having too much fun to give you a hard time." With those words he urged Shandy into a gallop and once more scattered the herd.

When the two had tired of their game, they contented themselves with meandering in and out of the shadows. The moon was high in the sky, casting a luminous glow over the whole world. A heavy layer of frost glistened like diamond crystals and tinkled into shards as the horses moved over the grass. The cold air hung thick and silent, broken only by an occasional owl or a low moo from the cows. Greg and Kelly were content to ride in silence, absorbing the beauty of the winter night.

Just as they were getting ready to turn back, Greg held his finger to his lips and signaled Kelly to stop. Pointing in the direction they had come from, he smiled. Looking up, Kelly saw three deer—two does and a buck—as they emerged from their woodland shelter. The buck had a huge rack of antlers and was keeping a careful eye on the mounted invaders in his pasture. The standoff continued until he was satisfied his charges were in no danger. Assured of safety, he lowered his head and began to paw the grass and eat.

As Kelly watched, she suddenly was aware that Greg had moved Shandy as close as possible to Crystal. A quickening of her pulse told her what was coming. Turning her head, she met Greg's eyes, just inches from her own. The feel of his lips on hers turned the frosty night into a wonderland. Their kisses were few and far between. Maybe that's what kept them so special.

"I've had a great night. Thanks for the surprise." Greg's voice was as warm as his eyes looking into hers.

Kelly didn't trust her voice, so she just smiled and reached for his hand. Silently they watched the deer until the creeping cold in their bodies told them they needed to head back.

• • •

It had taken two cups each of hot chocolate to warm their frigid bodies when they returned to the barn. The horses had gotten double portions of carrots and apples and were happily munching hay when they left. Kelly, unable to deceive Grand- daddy when he had asked them where they rode, had confessed their cowboy antics of the evening. Granddaddy had merely laughed and entertained them with more stories of his riding adventures when he was younger.

Sitting in the car in the driveway, Kelly was reluc- tant to leave the magic of the evening. Greg switched off the car and turned to her.

"How about if we pray for Brent?" he asked rather suddenly. "I'm really worried about him. You don't think he'd do something stupid, do you? He seems to be getting more depressed."

Kelly nodded. "I know what you mean. Julie is really worried about him, too. He won't tell any of us what's going on. Praying seems like a good idea."

They spent the next few minutes praying for their friend, and then Greg walked her to the door. "If I come in, I'm not going to want to leave."

Kelly gave him an understanding smile. "No problem. We can say good-night here."

Greg hugged her close.

"Thanks again for a great night," he whispered gently in her ear. He walked to his car and drove away.

TEN

A cacophony of sounds, sights, and smells assaulted Kelly's senses as she strode through the gym doors Saturday afternoon. Carpet had been rolled out on the floor and walls set up to convert the court into an indoor soccer arena. People were everywhere—boys in soccer suits of all colors representing their teams, coaches giving last-minute advice and strategy, and cheering fans in the stands. There was a fierce game going on when she walked in, but a quick glance assured her that it wasn't the Kingsport team. The first order of business was to find Greg and Julie. Scanning the crowds, she located them just as Greg looked down and saw her. Waving broadly, he jumped up and picked his way down the bleachers to join her.

Taking her hand, he began to climb back up. "Let's go. Brent's next game is supposed to start in ten minutes. So far they're still in the running. The last game was close, but they pulled it off in the last couple of minutes. Martin and Janie showed up a little while ago. They went to get something to drink, and then they're coming back to join us.

Steve, Joe, and Carrie are roaming around, too. I'm saving seats until the game starts. If our team wins this one, they'll have a thirty-minute break, and then they'll play the championship match."

Kelly nodded as she followed him through the mass of people populating the stands.

Julie gave her a quick hug as she sat down. "It's about time you got here! The last game was *so* close. Greg and the other guys just laughed at me when I got so excited. I need some female support!"

"You got me. This is going to be fun." Kelly sat down and looked around. As she absorbed all the action, she gradually felt the excitement invading her being. By the time the game started, she was pumped and ready to go. She cheered loudly as the boys from Kingsport High ran to take their places on the field.

"Here's hoping they win!"

Kelly looked up as Martin raised his cup of Coke and then sat down next to her.

"Hi, Martin. Hi, Janie."

"Hi, yourself, Kelly."

The whistle blew and their attention was riveted on the action unfolding on the field. Kingsport took an early lead when Brent stole a ball from an opponent. Racing down the field, he passed it off and then faked his way into a scoring position. The ball was passed off twice more before he connected and scored.

Kelly, Greg, and Julie jumped to their feet in wild cheering as he grinned in their direction and then took off down the field again.

"Boy, he needed that one!" Greg sat back down with a satisfied look.

"What do you mean? How's it been going today?" Kelly asked.

Greg shrugged. "He's having a hard day. One minute he seems focused and pulls off great plays like that one. The next minute he seems to be in another world."

"He's given up a couple of balls that led to points for the other team," Julie added. "That's why they almost lost the last game. But then he pulled through in the last minute and passed off a brilliant shot that led to a goal. It's nerve-wracking to watch him. It's almost like two people playing. I've been watching him on the bench. He seems really frustrated."

They turned their attention back to the game just in time to watch Kingsport's goalie block a goal attempt and send the ball flying back down the field. For the next two quarters there was no scoring as the boys battled it out on the field.

"At least Brent seems to be in good control."

"Huh?" Kelly made no pretense of being an expert on soccer. She wasn't sure what Greg was talking about.

Martin answered her question. "I coached soccer for a couple of years while I was in seminary," he said. "Control means being able to stop or change the direction of the ball whether it's in the air, bouncing on the ground, or just rolling along. It's a tough skill to master. It requires a combination of great reflexes, good balance, and body control. It takes a long time to become really good. Brent has a natural talent. He's been playing a long time, but there are college kids who aren't as good as he is."

Brent edged into a scoring position. One of his teammates, seeing him open, passed the ball to him at a high speed. The pass was perfect but when Brent moved to receive it, the ball hit the outside of his foot too hard and bounced off. Kelly heard Greg groan beside her. One of Olympic's players was right there and deftly stole the ball away. Brent, instead of immediately chasing him, slowed down and shook his head in frustration. Caught by surprise, Kingsport's boys moved quickly to the defensive, but it was not enough. Seconds later Olympic scored a goal and the game was tied.

"The coach is pulling him out of the game," Julie said.

Greg turned his attention to the Kingsport bench where Brent was now seated, frustration and anger obvious on his face.

The last quarter netted a game-winning goal for Kingsport, but Brent was never sent back in. Greg kept an eye on Brent as Coach Mullins talked with him. Brent just kept nodding his head and occasionally shrugged his shoulders. Once he looked up and saw Greg watching him, but he immediately turned his gaze away before he saw the thumbs-up signal Greg flashed him.

"I sure hope they let him play in the championship game," Julie spoke with concern. "He'll be crushed if they leave him on the bench."

Greg shook his head. "I don't think they'll bench him. He's having a hard day, but he's the best player they've got. They're going to need him. The coach is probably just giving him a break."

Thirty minutes later Kingsport took the field against their arch-rival, Clinton High. Everyone had known the contest would ultimately be between these two schools. It promised to be a great game. The usual milling around of the crowd stopped. The concession stand was empty as everyone focused on the field.

Brent was among the starting players.

The first three quarters resulted in a scoreless game, but the playing was superb. There was a constant change of ball control as players feinted, passed, and stole with skill.

"Brent is doing a great job!" Martin was as involved in the game as Greg, Kelly, and Julie. "He seems to have shaken off whatever was bugging him earlier. He looks like his confidence is back."

Greg glanced at him. How had Martin known something was bugging Brent?

Martin caught his look. "It's my job to know when kids are struggling with something. Is Brent okay?"

Just then a roar went up from the crowd as Clinton drove in for the first goal of the game. Greg's attention returned to the game, and he merely nodded. He and Martin could talk later.

With only one minute remaining, Kingsport still had not scored. Greg watched as Brent focused his attention on Coach Mullins, nodding at the signal given him. His face tightened in concentration until his eyes focused on movement along the railing. Greg followed his gaze just in time to see Mr. Jackson walk in with Allison and Mrs. Jackson turn in anger and walk away. Flashing his eyes back to Brent's face, Greg saw pain mix with the frustration. Just then the ball was thrown into play from the sidelines.

Brent focused soon enough to head the ball on to a teammate. Turning, he raced down the field looking for an open space. Five of his teammates joined with him in an effort to create the hole he needed. The crowd roared as the ball was passed at lightening speed down the field. The ball had just reached the far corner when Brent broke free in front of the goal. Aaron drew back his leg and with a powerful kick sent the ball soaring toward his teammate. Brent's face was intense—a little too intense. Racing into position, he snapped his upper body forward and headed the ball. Had Brent waited two more seconds, it would have been an incredible shot. As it was, it soared harmlessly past the goal just as the buzzer sounded.

The Clinton contingency roared as their team broke into celebration. Greg, Kelly, and Julie only had eyes for Brent. Despondency blanketed his features. Lowering his head, Brent turned and walked from the field. A couple of his teammates patted his shoulders in consolation, but he just shrugged them off and went into the locker room.

Greg exchanged concerned looks with his friends. "This wasn't exactly what he needed. I'm afraid this is going to make things worse."

Kelly and Julie nodded, and then began to make their way through the crowd to meet Brent when he came out. Greg saw Mr. Jackson try and get his son's attention without success. The next time he looked, Mr. Jackson and Allison were gone.

When Brent joined Julie, Kelly, and Greg forty-five minutes later, he acted as if nothing had happened. Greg was confused. Was Brent really that good an actor? Or did he just not care? After his attitude about flunking his tests, maybe Brent didn't care. But Greg knew better than that. Brent had played his heart out. Greg was convinced that Brent's loss of concentration when his mother walked out had caused his timing to be off. Maybe he just didn't want his friends to know what he was really feeling. After his successful attempts to brush them off for the last couple of weeks, Greg decided that was probably more the truth.

There were a few comments made about the tournament, but it was obvious Brent didn't want to talk about it. The conversation turned to other things.

"The weather is supposed to be great tonight." Julie tried to lighten the atmosphere. "Looks like we're still on for our hike and campfire out at the barn. What time are you picking us up tonight, Greg?"

"I'll be there between seven and seven-thirty. I'll come by and pick you up first, Brent."

Brent responded with a listless nod.

• • •

Brent walked into his house expecting to find his mother waiting for him. He was sure she was going to have angry words about his father showing up at the game with Allison. He was dreading it. As usual, he wouldn't know what to say, and he would just listen as his mother spewed her bitterness. He felt sorry for her, but he didn't know how to help.

He was surprised to find the house empty. Laying down his gym bag, he moved into the kitchen to fix a drink. She must have gone over to one of her friend's houses to unload her bitterness there, he thought. Taking a glass down from the cabinet, he filled it with ice and then tea. Tipping the glass he downed one, two, then three glasses of the refreshing liquid. His thirst finally quenched, he turned toward the refrigerator again. He was starving. A quick look told him that, as usual, his mom hadn't done much grocery shopping that week. The days of regular cooked meals had vanished with his father. Usually Brent just grabbed a sandwich or fixed a frozen meal. Today there was no bread, no frozen meals. Settling for a couple of apples and a glass of milk, he moved over to the kitchen table. Only then did he notice the note propped up against the napkin holder.

> *Dear Brent,*
>   *I've decided to leave on my business trip early. I'll be back late tomorrow night. There is money in the dresser drawer. If you need more, call your father. He always has plenty.*
>
>   *Love,*
>   *Mom*

Brent scowled, crumpled the note, and tossed it into the trash can. Why couldn't she just give it a rest? He polished off the apples, drained the milk, and then noticed the blinking light on the answering machine. Walking over, he flipped the switch to play. Maybe Mom had changed her mind and was coming back home, he silently hoped. Usually he didn't mind being alone, but he wasn't so sure it was a good idea tonight. Even though he was going out with Greg, Julie, and Kelly, he kind of wanted her there.

> *Hi, Brent. This is Dad. That was a great game today. Sorry about the last goal attempt. Another couple of seconds and the header would have been perfect. Hey, you gave it your best shot. I wanted to talk to you after, but I'm heading out of town on business. And I wasn't sure if your mother was still around. I didn't want to make her any angrier. You know how she is about Allison. Have a great night. I'll try to catch up with you later.*

Brent's scowl deepened. Why couldn't they have their own war and leave him out of the line of fire? It was hard enough trying to keep both of them happy. He was tired of being the middle man to receive and deliver their shots to each other.

Brent wandered into his bedroom and threw himself across his bed. Looking at his clock, he noticed that he had an hour before Greg would be by to pick him up. Lying there, Brent allowed his mind to wander. He had been so sure about making that final goal today. If his concentration hadn't been blown by seeing his mom walk out, maybe... Flunking those tests had been stupid. If he wanted to get into a good school, his junior year was really important. He would have to work like a dog next semester to make his yearly average a good one. The trouble was that he just didn't care... He still couldn't believe his father had let Allison join them in D.C.

He had felt so humiliated in front of Greg. And then to blow up and let Greg know all the things he was feeling. How could he have been so stupid? This was his problem, and he just needed to handle it. No one else needed to know what a screwed-up mess his family was . . . And Christmas. Only six more days. Would this year be as bad as last? His mother had been angry because his father had wanted to see him and his mother knew that Allison would be there. His father had been equally angry at his mother for being angry, so he hadn't brought Greg home until two hours after the planned time, messing up his mom's dinner plans. This year looked like it might only be worse.

Brent's room darkened along with his thoughts. Another look at the clock told him Greg was supposed to pick him up in thirty minutes. Rolling over, he picked up the phone and dialed.

"Hello."

"Greg. This is Brent."

"Hey. I'm just finishing up dinner. I'll be there in about twenty-five minutes."

In the background Brent could hear the noisy chatter of Greg's big, happy family. "Don't bother coming by to pick me up. I'm really beat from the soccer tournament. I must not be over whatever was making me feel bad last night. Would you call Julie for me?"

"You're bugging out on us again?" Greg couldn't hide the frustration in his voice.

Brent didn't even care enough to defend himself. "Yeah, I guess I am. Pretty worthless, aren't I? Sorry. I'll see you later. Maybe." Rolling over, he hung up the phone and resumed staring at the ceiling.

You're screwing up everything. Greg's mad at you now, and Julie is going to be really hurt that you're backing out on her again. What's the use? You've messed up everything, and there's really no way to put it back together. You're always going to be in the middle of your folks. You've tried to help, but it hasn't done any good.

Brent's black thoughts deepened and finally swallowed him. Rising from his prone position on the bed, he moved with resolution toward his mother's bathroom.

• • •

Greg shook his head as he hung up the phone.

"Problems, Greg?"

"Brent is backing out of our double-date again tonight, Dad. And I feel really bad because I'm mad at him." Greg frowned. "His voice bothered me. It sounded so dead. I wish he would just shake off whatever's eating him. I don't believe he's sick. He just doesn't want to go, so he's making up an excuse."

Greg's father nodded sympathetically. "He probably just feels bad about blowing the game today. At least that's how he probably sees it. That's tough for a competitive player like Brent."

Greg nodded but felt a nagging doubt in the back of his mind. Should he go over to Brent's? Thoughts of the girls pushed that from his mind. He needed to call Kelly and come up with an alternative plan so he could tell Julie something when he called her. He didn't want to leave Julie stranded for another night.

She was already confused enough by Brent's behavior. Brent was lucky Julie was putting up with him.

Kelly picked up on the third ring. "Hello."

"Kelly, it's Greg. Brent is bugging out on us again."

"What's wrong this time?"

"Oh, who knows what's really wrong," Greg said in frustration. "He won't talk to anybody. His excuse is that he's too tired from the soccer tournament and not feeling real well. He also left me the job of calling Julie again, but I don't want to until we come up with an alternative plan. I think we should can the hike and campfire and do something she won't feel uncomfortable joining us on."

Greg's dad walked by the phone again. "We're leaving now, son. We're going to drop the girls off at their friends' houses, and then we're headed to the movies. We'll be home by about eleven-thirty."

"Okay, Dad. I'll be in by midnight." Waving a hand, he returned to his conversation with Kelly.

For the next twenty minutes they bounced options back and forth until they finally decided to drive around town for the "Tacky Christmas Light" tour. Kelly hadn't done it in years, and this was Greg's first Christmas in Kingsport. She convinced Greg that everyone needed to experience it at least once. After they had seen everything, they would go back to Kelly's house to watch old Christmas movies and eat cookies by the fire.

"Why don't I give Julie a call?" Kelly suggested. "I think I can convince her that we really want her along. I don't want her staying at home tonight. In fact, I think I'll ask her to spend the night. We can get up in the morning and go to church."

"Thanks. I wasn't looking forward to calling her again. I'll be there in about fifteen minutes. I just need to do a few things."

"Okay. See you soon."

Greg double-checked to make sure all the doors were locked, grabbed a couple of bags of chips for them to munch while they were driving around, and pulled his coat off the hat rack in the hall. His hand was on the doorknob when the phone rang. Glancing at it, he shrugged and began to open the door. But something stopped him. Staying where he was, he decided to at least listen to the message on the answering machine. Maybe it was Kelly calling back. He waited for the machine to click on, deliver its message, and then record the caller. Brent's voice filled the room.

"Hey, Greg. Are you still there? This is Brent."

Greg was struck by his friend's tone. Moving quickly across the room, he picked up the phone. "Yeah, Brent. I'm still here. I was just getting ready to leave. Did you change your mind about joining us?"

Greg heard Brent's voice catch. "I've done something really stupid." He was making no effort to hide his fear.

Greg's heartbeat quickened. "What's wrong? What did you do?"

"I don't know what made me do it. Take the pills, I mean. I know I took too many..." Brent's voice trailed off. "I don't want to die. You've got to help me..."

Greg's mind and heart began to race at the same time. What was he supposed to do? "I'll be right there, Brent. I'm going to call for help first. Hang in there. I'll be there!" Slamming down the phone, Greg's mind searched for what to do.

Call 911.

The message sounded in his heart like a trumpet. Yanking the phone back up, he punched out the numbers and waited breathlessly. When the operator came on the line, he started talking, "My friend. He's taken too many pills. He needs help." Greg's voice was frantic.

The voice coming back over the line was calm and soothing. "Where is your friend?"

"He's at his house. I'm going over there now."

"Where does your friend live? We'll get some help to him right away."

Of course they would need to know where Brent lived! Greg knew the street, but he didn't know the number. Grabbing a phone book, he feverishly flipped pages. "Chambers Road. 8023 Chambers Road. It's a white house with blue shutters. That's where he is."

"What's your name?"

"What do you need my name for?" Greg felt himself begin to get hysterical. "We don't have time for this! He could be dying!"

"Don't panic," the operator said. "I've already dispatched the paramedics. Now, what's your name?"

"Greg. My name is Greg Adams. His name is Brent Jackson. He's there alone. I've got to get there. He just called me."

"Okay, Greg," the operator's voice remained calm, "if you get there before the paramedics, just try and talk to him. Do you know what kind of pills he took?"

"No. I didn't think to ask him."

"No problem. There's no reason you should have known to do that. Since we don't know what he took, we don't know how it will affect him. See if you can find the bottle he got the pills from. And if he's sleepy, try to keep him awake and talking. Someone will be there as soon as possible."

Greg slammed down the phone and ran from the house.

ELEVEN

Greg jumped from his car and ran to Brent's darkened house. There was not a single light on. What if the door was locked? he worried. Would Brent be able to let him in? He breathed a sigh of relief when the doorknob turned under his hand. Fearing the worst, he stepped in and flipped the light switch beside the door. Blazing light revealed nothing but an empty room.

"Brent!" He raised his voice to fill the house. There was no answer. Was he too late? Racing through the house, he turned on every light until the house shone brilliantly onto the yard and street. At least the paramedics would have no trouble finding it. Plunging down the hall, he finally discovered Brent in his mother's bedroom.

"Brent!" One glance told him his friend was in trouble. His eyes were open, but the eyelids were flickering with sleep. He was lying on the bed and seemed to barely notice that Greg was in the room. Kneeling down beside his friend, Greg shook his shoulders. There was no response. Remembering the 911 operator's words, he shook his shoulders harder. "Brent! Can you hear me?" Only then did Brent's eyes turn his way and attempt to focus. Still he said nothing—just stared. Greg's heart was beating so hard he thought it would jump from his chest. What if his friend died while he was there? Why had Brent done this? Greg groaned in frustration and pain.

He continued to shake Brent's shoulders and call his name while he allowed his eyes to roam the room in search of the pill bottle. Finally he spotted an open bottle on Mrs. Jackson's dresser. Jumping up, he grabbed it and read the label: *Elavil*. The bottle had his mother's name on it. As Greg laid it on the nightstand to give to the paramedics, his eyes were drawn to a folded piece of typing paper. *Mom* was scrawled in Brent's familiar handwriting. Just then he heard the ambulance siren as the squad entered the neighborhood. Grabbing the sheet of paper, he stuffed it in his pocket. He would give it to Brent's mom later.

He ran to the front door just as the ambulance roared up the driveway. He beckoned to the paramedics running through the yard. Plunging into the house, they followed him down the hallway to the bed where Brent was lying, more and more unresponsive. He made no effort to acknowledge the paramedics when they shook his shoulders and yelled at him.

Greg stepped back to allow them to work and tried to answer the questions fired at him.

"Do you know what he took?"

Greg reached over, grabbed the bottle, and handed it to the lead paramedic.

Glancing at it, the paramedic stuck it in his pocket. "How long ago did he take them?"

Greg shook his head. "I have no idea. He called me about twenty minutes ago. He told me he'd done it, but he didn't say when he took them."

The paramedic nodded and then went into action. His orders came fast and furious. "I don't know how long we have with this one. He took Elavil. He probably only has two hours from the time he took them. Sam, go get the gurney. I'll get his vital signs."

Sam ran for the door as the lead paramedic searched for a pulse. His concerned look only deepened the dread in Greg's heart. He knew it would take them a couple of minutes to get Brent into the ambulance, so he ran down the hall to the kitchen. Grabbing the phone, he punched out Kelly's number.

"Hello."

"Kelly, this is Greg. Listen. You have to get your folks and come to the hospital. Brent tried to kill himself with an overdose." He didn't slow down at Kelly's gasp over the phone. "My folks are at the Westmont Theater. Will you stop by there and let them know what's going on? I want them to be there. I have to go now. The paramedics are taking him out." Slamming down the phone, he ran out the door behind the stretcher.

The lead paramedic—Greg read Gordon on his name tag—remembered he was there. "Where are this kid's parents?"

"I don't know. I don't know his father's phone number, and I have no idea where his mom is."

Gordon nodded. "You look a little too shook to be driving. You might as well come with us."

Those were exactly the words Greg wanted to hear. He jumped into the ambulance behind the paramedics. Finding a little seat out of the way, he remained quiet as once more the paramedics seemed to forget he was there.

When they had the gurney secure, Gordon began to fire more instructions. "Sam, get an IV into him. We need to start getting sodium bicarbonate into his system. I know this is your first suicide attempt, but get used to it." Gordon looked grim. "Over a hundred kids a week kill themselves in this country. Over a thousand a day try but don't succeed. A lot of the kids who try and don't succeed just mess themselves up for life. They think they're choosing an easy way out, but they're wrong."

Greg watched as Sam moved to hook up the IV. "The sodium bicarbonate is going to soak up the acid in his stomach, right? I saw the bottle the kid gave you. Elavil can cause cardiac arrest, can't it?"

"Yeah. That's why I'm hooking him up to the heart monitor. I wish I knew how long ago he'd taken them. He lost consciousness just as we were taking him out. The pattern is for his heartbeat to become irregular, then he'd start to have seizures before he went into cardiac arrest. I only hope we got to him in time."

Sam turned his attention to Greg for a moment and tried to give him an assuring smile. "You did the right thing calling 911 before you went over to his house. A few minutes could make the difference. Do you know why he did it?"

"I know he's been pretty stressed out lately over things in his family," Greg answered shakily, "but he wouldn't talk to me about it. I never dreamed he would try to kill himself. I knew he was depressed, but I thought Christmas break would help him. He messed up in a soccer game today. We were supposed to go out tonight, but at the last minute he called to say he couldn't go. Thirty minutes later he called back to say he'd taken the pills and asked me to help him. Why would he try to kill himself?" Greg could feel the tears welling up in his eyes.

"I don't know what made him do it, but I know one thing: It's not your fault," Sam spoke firmly. "Sometimes the signs are obvious, sometimes they're not. He made a bad choice. You're not responsible for that. All you can do now is be his friend. He's going to need that."

Greg nodded and continued to watch Brent. He was frightened by his pale face and shallow breathing. What if they hadn't gotten to him in time? "What are they going to do to him when we get to the hospital?"

"First thing they'll do is monitor everything and hook him up to a fresh IV," Sam replied. "Then they will pump his stomach. The nurse will take a tube and force it up his nose, through his sinus passages, and down his throat into his stomach. His nose will be sore when he wakes up, but at least he won't feel it at the time. It's incredibly painful. Most suicide attempts from overdoses are still awake when they get to the hospital.

"Once the tube is down there, they flip on the motor to the suction that will pump his stomach of the pills. They'll also have to put a tube down to his lungs to protect his air passages in case his gag reflexes aren't working right. Once they've pumped out the pills, they'll reverse the flow and pump liquid charcoal down into his stomach to neutralize the acids and poison. He'll be pretty sick for a while after he wakes up. The stomach doesn't appreciate charcoal being pumped into it, so its natural reaction is to get rid of it."

Greg could feel his stomach churning as he digested the information. If Brent could have only known the consequences of his actions.

It took only ten minutes to arrive at the hospital. With lights flashing and siren wailing, they pulled up to the emergency room door. Gordon turned to Greg with final instructions. "You'll need to stay in the waiting room for a while. Give them all the information you can. Then see if you can find his parents. They need to be here. And if you're the praying type, I'd pray."

"I've been doing that ever since he called," Greg said. "I'll try to find his parents. Thank you so much."

Sam and Gordon nodded, wheeled the gurney into the emergency room, and then stepped aside as hospital personnel took over. Greg watched as they sped Brent down the hall and through the swinging emergency room doors. With a heavy heart, he turned toward the reception desk. Ten minutes later he had given them all the information he could and was standing in the middle of the room trying to figure out how to contact Brent's parents. Just then he looked up to see his own parents, Kelly, and her parents burst through the doors. Looking around, they caught sight of him and rushed over.

His mother was the first to reach him. Without saying a word, she wrapped her arms around him and gave him a big hug. She seemed to sense the drain the night's experience had been on him. Greg allowed himself a few moments to receive her comfort, but then he pulled his shoulders back and straightened up. There was still a lot to be done. He knew they were going to have a lot of questions, but first . . .

"We need to try and find Brent's parents. His father has an unlisted number, and I don't know where his mom is. The doctors really need to talk to them."

"Scott and I will figure out what to do," Greg's dad spoke first. "You've done enough for one night. I imagine we still have a long haul before us. You stay here in case there's news. We'll find his parents."

Greg nodded, glad to have the problem taken from his hands. Finding a sofa, he settled down with his mother, Kelly, and Peggy. Kelly took his hand, and they sat quietly for a few minutes. They sensed his need to gather his thoughts and emotions.

His mother finally broke the silence. "Can you talk about it?"

Greg turned to her and relayed the events of the night. Their faces tightened in concern as he told them what the paramedics had said about the pills and what the consequences could be. His mother wiped tears from her face as he talked about searching the house for his friend and trying to follow the 911 operator's instructions to keep Brent awake. He also told them about the medical procedures that would be used to try and keep Brent alive.

Kelly's handhold grew tighter and tighter as he talked. Just as Greg finished his story, Julie and her parents came running through the door. Julie rushed up to Kelly with a tearful face. "We just got home and found the message. Right after you called the first time, I went out to eat with my folks. I was mad because Brent stood me up again tonight, and I knew it would be too hard seeing you and Greg together. I should have called him. Maybe if I'd just called he wouldn't have tried to do it!" Fresh sobs engulfed her as she wailed out, "Is he dead? Where is he?"

Kelly jumped up and wrapped her arms around her friend. "As far as we know he's still alive." Quickly she filled Julie and her parents in on what had been going on.

Peggy spoke up from her seat on the sofa. "All we can do is wait. And pray. Scott and Eric, Greg's dad, are trying to locate Brent's parents. Why don't we spend some time praying?"

For the next twenty minutes their little group huddled in chairs around the sofa, held hands, and prayed for Brent. When they lifted their heads, Greg felt a peace for the first time that night. They still didn't know anything, but once more he was aware that God was in control.

Opening doors caught his attention. Looking up, he saw Martin and Janie stride into the room.

"I called them," Peggy answered Greg's unspoken question. She relieved Greg by filling the couple in on the situation. Just as she finished speaking, Eric and Scott returned to the group.

"We got in touch with both of his parents," Eric said with relief. "Since we couldn't reach either one of them at home, we tracked down their bosses at work to see if they were on business trips. They were. The bosses were able to give us their itineraries. We called the hotels where they were staying. They both were shocked. They've gotten early morning flights out and will be here by noon. I told them we would call again as soon as we knew anything. His mother has already called the hospital and given them permission to do whatever they need to."

"Thanks, Dad. I *never* would have found them!" Greg said with deep appreciation. Looking around at the group, he realized how fortunate he, Kelly, and Julie were to have their parents. What would he do if his family were more like Brent's?

"Are you the folks here with Brent Jackson?"

Everyone jumped to their feet as a white-coated doctor strode up and addressed their group.

"We are, doctor." Greg's father took control. "My name is Eric Adams. My son, Greg, was in the ambulance when they brought him in. Brent called him after he took the pills."

"Brent is very lucky he called Greg when he did. His heart had begun to beat irregularly by the time we got him in ER. Another thirty or forty minutes and it would have been too late. He would have gone into cardiac arrest. I doubt we could have saved him."

Greg shuddered as he heard the words.

"He's going to be okay," the doctor continued. "We've pumped everything out, and his vital signs have stabilized. He's going to be very sick and miserable for a while, but he's going to make it. The thing to do now is to figure out why he did it and try to keep it from happening again. We'll keep him here for a couple of days to monitor him and have some psychiatric evaluation done. The doctors and his parents will have to make the decision whether to put him in the psychiatric hospital for help or not."

Julie gasped, "You mean he can't come home when he's better?"

The doctor's voice was grave. "I don't know. It will depend on what they find out. Most kids who come in here like this end up in the hospital for a couple of weeks at least. We don't want them to try it again before they get help."

The adults nodded their heads in understanding, but Greg, Kelly, and Julie were stunned. What would Brent do if he had to spend two weeks in the hospital? That meant missing Christmas—everything.

"When can we see him?" Greg asked.

"He just regained consciousness a few minutes ago. It will be several hours before he'll feel like having company."

"Can I stay here for the night? In his room, I mean, once I get to go in?"

The doctor fixed him with a kind gaze. "You're a good friend, young man. I think Brent will be glad to have you. If it's okay with your parents, it's okay with me. But no more than just one of you."

Greg nodded eagerly, relieved to know he would be able to be with Brent. Maybe his presence would make up for the fact he hadn't been able to keep Brent from trying to commit suicide.

"It's not your fault, you know." Martin's voice sounded in the room as the doctor turned to walk away.

Greg turned and looked into his caring eyes. Now that he knew Brent was okay, he could feel his control slipping. Tears filled his eyes. He had been so scared. Out of the corner of his eye he could see tears slipping down Kelly's and Julie's faces. "Why did he do it, Martin?" The question had haunted him all night and was wrung from deep inside his aching heart.

The rest of the group was silent as Martin searched for the right words. "What drives people to try and kill themselves is different for everyone. But I think I can give you some idea of what he must have been feeling. When I was seventeen, I tried to commit suicide."

Greg's face registered disbelief. "You? You tried to kill yourself? I never knew that."

"I've talked to the youth group about it before, but not since you and Kelly have started coming," Martin said.

Choosing his words carefully he continued, "When I was fourteen some friends introduced me to the drug scene. I had been a pretty good kid until then, but I really wanted to fit in. It started out with just an occasional joint. The sensation of getting high was fun, and I was a part of the crowd. I began to get more rebellious, and fights with my parents became a common thing. I was sure they could never understand me. Gradually the drug use intensified. When I was almost seventeen, some friends gave me some bad stuff that sent me on a really rough trip. When I came down, I was miserably sick. Every time I ate, I would get sick.

"When I didn't get better, my parents took me to the doctor. They discovered I had a bleeding ulcer. I was hospitalized for two weeks. I got behind in school, my friends forgot I existed, and I felt horrible about all the pain I was putting my family through. Once I got home, I was still really sick. It took two months before I started to gain weight again. All the things that had made me take drugs in the first place were still eating at me. I was convinced there was no reason to live. I was also sure no one would miss me if I killed myself. It was like I was in a huge dark tunnel, and all I could see was blackness swallowing who I was. I just got tired. Tired of fighting it. Tired of trying to believe there was light somewhere if I just kept going. I allowed darkness to win.

"One day I waited until my parents had gone to work and my brothers and sisters had gone to school, and then I went into my parents' bathroom and slit my wrists. I wanted them to find my body there and feel as bad as I did. Only right after I'd done it and saw the blood everywhere, I realized I didn't really want to die. I called 911, and they got to me in time. I had to spend a month in a psychiatric hospital. Shortly after that I became a Christian and God started to work things out."

"But Brent's a Christian already." Greg was still confused. "Why would he do it?"

Martin smiled gently. "That's a good question. Again, each person has their own pain that drives them over the edge. We'll know more about what pushed Brent over that edge when we talk to him. Many times people leave a note..."

"A note! I forgot about the note!" Fishing in his pockets, Greg pulled out the white sheet of paper with *Mom* written on it. "Brent wrote it to his mother. He left it on the nightstand beside where she would have found him." The picture in his mind made Greg shudder. "Do you think it's okay if we read it?"

"It could give you an idea of how to talk to him later. I think it's okay to read it. You can give it to his mom when she gets here tomorrow." Nodding heads confirmed Martin's words.

Greg unfolded the paper and read out loud the words he found there.

> *Darkness*
> *Swallowing all that I am*
> *Leaving nothing*
> *Nothing to live for*
> *I bow to the darkness.*
> *I stand back and let it take me*
> *I go to join it*
> *To rest in it*
> *The pain*
> *Swallowed by the darkness*
> *Can consume me no more*
> *I am at peace*
> *I am dead.*

Mom,
> *I couldn't take it anymore. I'm a failure as a son. I can't make you or Dad happy. I'm too tired to try anymore. I'm blowing it at school. My insides are ripped up. I need peace. I hope God will forgive me. I love you.*

Tell Dad I love him, too. You'll be better off without me.

Brent

P.S. In case you care, there is a notebook in my room full of things I've written. That's all I have to give you. I know it's not much. Bye.

The group was silent as they attempted to absorb the impact of Brent's words. Each one of them struggled with trying to comprehend his pain.

Martin's voice was soft. "Sometimes our pain is so great that all we want to do is run from it. We're convinced that not even God can help us. And the world says that suicide is an easy option. A lot of people choose that way to escape their pain.

"Brent said he hoped God would forgive him. I don't believe suicide is an unforgivable sin. Only Brent and God could have known where his heart was if he had died. But I do believe that God weeps when his children decide to end their lives that way. God has so many plans for them. He has so much beauty he wants to pour into their lives if they will bring him the pain instead of running from it.

"Brent wasn't responsible for the turmoil in his family. He didn't cause it, and he couldn't control it. But he could run to God and learn how to let him make sense out of all of it. Just because you're a Christian, just because you have asked Jesus into your life doesn't mean you won't struggle with pain. And it doesn't mean that you automatically know how to give your problems to Jesus and let him carry them for you. It takes time, and it takes effort to

know God in an intimate way—in a way that will
carry you through the hard times. Brent hadn't
learned how to do that yet. Thank God he'll have
another chance."

Julie broke the silence that followed Martin's
words. "What can we do to help him?"

"I think there is a lot you—all of us—can do to
help him," Martin answered gently. "The most
important thing is to continue loving him. He needs
to be loved and supported and reassured we will
stand with him. I'm sure that his doctors and parents will determine he needs to be in counseling.
The notebook he mentioned in his letter will help
his counselor. I had one of those, too. I didn't know
how to talk about my problems, but I could write my
feelings. We need to pray that Brent will learn how
to open up and talk about his pain instead of bot-
tling it up. Once he does, we need to listen, not
judge, just listen. Often, just talking about it eases
the pressure. The problem might still be there, but
it's not so bad when a friend knows and is sharing it
with us."

Martin paused, choosing his next words carefully.
"It would be easy to try and ignore what he's done
tonight," he continued at last. "But that won't help.
It needs to be talked about. And at the right time
each of you—Greg, Kelly, Julie—you need to tell
him how what he tried made you feel. Most suicidal
people don't stop to think about the pain that family
and friends will carry through their whole lives if
their attempt is successful. All they can think about
is their own pain. Brent needs to understand what
he has done to each of you. But it can't be done as a

way of getting back at him. It needs to be done in love, and it needs to be done at the right time when it will help him and not make him feel worse."

"He will feel very awkward for a while," Peggy added. "All of us can do a lot to make him feel loved. I have great hopes his parents will work together to ease the strain caused by the bitterness of their divorce. In the meantime, all of us can make him feel a part of our families. He's alive, but he still has to learn to deal with what made him want to kill himself in the first place."

● ● ●

Two hours later a nurse walked down the hall and called for Greg. He jumped up to meet her.

"I'm Greg Adams. Can I go see Brent now?"

"You can. He's pretty miserable, but I think it would do him good to have company. He won't feel like talking I don't think, but just having you there will help. And the doctor said only one visitor until his folks get here tomorrow." Her concerned glance roved over the group assembled in the waiting room.

Greg's father spoke, "Now that we know he's okay, the rest of us are going to go on home. We were just waiting with my son." Slipping his arm around Greg's shoulder, he said, "I'll be praying for you, son. And I'm proud of you. You were a good friend tonight."

Greg made no attempt to hide the tears in his eyes as the group exchanged hugs and left the waiting area. Turning, he followed the nurse down the hall.

T W E L V E

What time did Brent come home from the hospital yesterday? I sent him a card that should have been waiting for him." Kelly spoke to Greg as they both stood in the barn grooming their horses.

"He got home about eleven yesterday morning. I spent most of the afternoon with him. He got your card. He seemed to really appreciate it. I think he's just glad to be home. He was pretty shook Sunday morning when he realized they weren't going to let him leave the hospital for a couple of days. At least he's talking, though. The scare of almost killing himself has made him realize he can't keep everything locked up inside. We've had some good talks."

This was the first time Kelly had gotten to have more than a brief phone conversation with Greg since Saturday night. He had been spending a lot of time with Brent at the hospital. She knew how much Brent needed him now. She had been busy trying to be supportive to Julie. Julie still felt Brent might not have tried suicide if she had done things differently. Kelly didn't know how to help her deal with her guilt and bad feelings. All she knew to do was be there and let her talk.

"He sure was happy when they decided he didn't have to go to the psychiatric hospital," Greg continued. "He told me the doctor came in and talked to him for a long time. Once he saw that Brent was really sorry for what he had done and that he really did want to live, they decided to let him go home. Brent seems determined to deal with everything. I think his parents are, too."

Greg stared thoughtfully into space as he ran a brush over Shandy's gleaming coat. "I like both of his parents. I don't think they knew what they were doing. They were so wrapped up in their own pain and their own desires that they didn't see how they were hurting Brent. What Brent did really shook them up. Mr. and Mrs. Jackson are talking to each other now and realizing they *were* putting Brent in the middle—expecting him to handle their problems and using him to make the other miserable. The whole family is going to start counseling after New Year's. They seem to want to work it out. Brent and his mom are coming to our house for Christmas dinner. He told them how hard it is to have to go to two places on Christmas, so he's going to spend it with his mom. He'll see his dad the day after. He seems happy about that."

"I'm so glad." Kelly's response was heartfelt. "I still shudder when I think how close he came to killing himself."

"Me, too. I've thought so many times about what would have happened if I had walked out the door to get you just thirty seconds earlier. I wouldn't have gotten his call, and he told me that he had never even thought of dialing 911. It's really good to know that God is in control of my life—and Brent's as well. I think he realizes God didn't want him to die. My dad says it will take him a while to work through everything, but at least he wants to now."

"Do you think we could have stopped Brent from trying to kill himself?" Kelly asked honestly. "Was there some way we should have known what was coming? I've been trying to make Julie feel better about it, but I've been wondering myself."

Greg spoke slowly. "I've been wondering that a lot, too. I talked to my dad and also mentioned it to Martin. Martin suggested a book for my dad and I to read together. It's on suicide—teen suicide, really. A lot of things are becoming clearer as I read it. I realize now that Brent was giving out some pretty clear signals. He was obviously depressed and really upset about his family situation. This book says that more than half of all suicidal kids give problems in their family as the reason. Another signal was when he flunked all those tests at school. He had quit caring then. When he blew the soccer game, he just gave up. I knew Brent had walls up. If I had known what was happening, I could have helped him more."

Kelly nodded thoughtfully before Greg contin-ued. "One thing my dad helped me see, though, is that I'm not responsible. Neither are you or Julie. Maybe we should have known the signs, but we're just kids. Hopefully, we'll recognize them if there's ever a next time. We'll at least be better prepared to help a friend. Most people just need someone to talk to. They want to know someone cares. But ulti-mately, Brent made a choice. We did *try* and talk to him, even though we didn't have any idea where this would end up. We couldn't *make* him talk. Feeling guilty about it won't help anyone. It's over. All we can do is be his friend and show him life is worth living. I think things will get a little bit easier now. His parents are trying. At least it's a start."

Kelly nodded and then remembered, "Oh, I forgot to tell you. My dad is calling your parents and Brent's and Julie's parents tonight. He and Peggy thought it would be a great idea if Brent and Julie joined our families when we go cross-country skiing after Christmas. I can't believe we leave in just three days. Anyway, Dad thought it would do Brent and Julie good to get away and have a change of pace, so he's going to ask."

Greg's smile lit the barn. "That would be great. I think that's just what Brent needs—to get out of town for a while and have a chance to be outside doing something. I hope his parents don't mind. Since we're leaving early, his dad won't get to see him the day after Christmas, but maybe they could work out something for Christmas Eve."

Kelly nodded hopefully and then silence fell between them as they finished brushing and tacking their horses up.

They had pulled Jackson and Ralph out of their stalls before Greg spoke again.

"What time is everyone supposed to be here?"

"Jim told us to all be ready to go by six-thirty. That way we can ride for about two hours and get back in plenty of time for the hot chocolate and food. I dropped off a plate of Peggy's cookies when I got here."

Greg nodded. "Yeah. I brought a plate of my mom's, too."

Jim Swanson, a boarder at the barn, had come up with the great idea of going Christmas caroling by horseback to the neighboring farms. Almost a dozen of the regulars at Porter's were enthusiastically joining him. He had devised a route through the woods and fields that would keep them off the roads and take them to about ten of the closest homes. Kelly was excited about doing it. She had once more talked Granddaddy into letting Brent and Julie use Ralph and Jackson, so they were coming as well. Wanting some time to talk with Greg, Kelly had asked him to pick her up early, though.

It didn't take long to groom and tack Ralph and Jackson. Glancing at her watch, Kelly noticed they still had thirty minutes before the others were due to arrive.

When Greg noticed her looking at her watch, he raised his eyebrows and grinned. "I'd say it's just enough time to hit the rope swing. What do you think?"

"I think you're reading my mind again! Let's go."

The rope swing had quickly become a favorite activity at the barn. Granddaddy had laughingly commented that he was probably never going to be able to use the pile of hay that served as the launch site for horse feed. Privately, Kelly hoped he never would. The swing was too much fun to mess up. Thankfully, it would be spring before the pile of hay became an issue. There was still plenty in the barn.

Kelly and Greg were laughing when they ran over to the barn to join Brent and Julie, after thirty minutes of fun-filled swinging. Kelly was breathless when she reached them.

"Your horses are ready," she said. "Greg and I got here early to take care of it." Walking over to Brent, she gave him a warm hug. He responded with a shy smile and hugged her back.

"Hi, Kelly. Thanks for your card."

"It's good to see you. I'm glad you're home. And I'm glad you could come tonight." Kelly tried hard to sound natural. Peggy and her father had told her how awkward he might feel and that just being natural would help him.

Julie broke into the conversation. "Kelly! Guess what?"

"Okay. What?"

"Your dad called just before we left. He asked us to go with you on your ski trip, and my mom and dad said yes! Brent gets to go, too!"

Kelly grinned. "That's great! I was hoping it was going to work out. We're going to have so much fun!"

As they talked about the ski trip, other cars began to pull up. Within twenty minutes the group was saddled and ready to ride.

Crystal was obviously excited about the opportunity for a late-night adventure. Kelly was sure she remembered their wild time of rounding up cattle the last time she had been out at night. Crystal was going to be disappointed if that's what she expected. Kelly laughed as her tall, black filly danced and pranced around the barnyard.

"You sure you can handle that horse?"

Kelly grinned at Jim's question. "She's just showing off. I like to let her have fun every now and again. She's still just a kid, you know. We need to be able to act crazy sometimes." To prove she had control over her filly, Kelly laid her hand on Crystal's neck and spoke softly. Crystal immediately stopped dancing and stood quietly with one ear cocked back for her next command.

Jim's expression registered his admiration. "That's some horse you have there!"

Kelly just smiled and nodded in agreement. She was well aware of how wonderful her dream horse was. She turned to make sure Julie and Brent were okay. They were standing right behind her, ready to head out the gate.

The whole group rode down the lane and then cut through a gate in the pasture to head over to the closest neighbor's house. They agreed to take turns opening gates through the night so no one had to do them all. Kelly was just amazed that Jim had taken the time to figure out the route. Jim had only been riding for two years, but the forty-five-year-old executive was quite comfortable on his seven-year-old quarter horse gelding. They made a good pair.

Everyone was quiet as they headed up to the first house. Moving their horses across the yard, they were careful not to trample any plants or bushes. Spreading out in a semi-circle around the porch, they sat in silence. At a nod from Jim, Greg dismounted and ran to the porch to ring the doorbell. As soon as he had pushed the button, he jumped off the porch, dashed to where Shandy was standing patiently, and vaulted back into the saddle. Just as he settled in, the porch light came on. That was their signal. Their voices rose as one in a chorus of "O

Come, All Ye Faithful." It was fun to see the delight on the neighbors' faces as they filed out onto the porch to listen.

Kelly looked around with a warm glow. The light from the rail porch spilled over into the yard and illuminated their group. As they sang, vapor rose from the horses' nostrils. Their occasional stomps lent the tinkle of bits and buckles as accompaniment. The still, frosty night air seemed to send their song ringing to the heavens. Amid applause and calls of "Merry Christmas!" they moved down the drive and continued on to the next house.

For two hours the riders meandered through woods and meadows until they located houses where they could sing. Only one family wasn't home. Undaunted, they had sung to the three horses watching from behind the fence. Their ringing neighs seemed to indicate approval. Laughing and talking, they left the last house and took the long way around to arrive back at the stables.

"Hey, look!" Kelly's cry alerted everyone as they followed her gaze into the sky.

"It's snowing!" Brent's voice yelled in triumph. "We're going to have a white Christmas."

"The first one in twenty-five years!" Julie was just as excited as Kelly.

Greg looked up in wonder and shook his head. "Man, this place is great. I thought I was going to hate North Carolina when I had to leave Texas. I sure was wrong. A white Christmas! And the snow will be perfect for our cross-country ski trip as well. We couldn't ask for anything better."

• • •

Brent raised up on one elbow and looked at Greg in the twin bed next to him in his bedroom. "I'm glad you could spend the night."

"Me, too. Have you looked out the window lately? The snow is still coming down really hard. Looks like the weatherman was on target when he predicted five inches. I bet the mountains get a lot more. The skiing should be great!"

For the next twenty minutes, the boys discussed the ski trip. When Brent fell silent, Greg asked him what he was thinking. He was learning it was a valuable question. It wasn't intrusive, and it gave the person the opportunity to either say something or dodge the question without seeming to.

Brent was quiet for a few minutes. Greg just waited. Brent would talk when he was ready. Finally he spoke.

"I guess I'm thinking I'm glad I'm not alone."

"How come?"

"Well, I don't think I want to die, but life still seems pretty overwhelming to me. It's like there's a battle going on inside of me. Part of me wants to live. The other part of me wants to die. One shouts louder than the other sometimes, and then they switch places."

Greg had spent some time with Martin on Sunday and had learned the value of asking questions. The youth director had told him that most people didn't want answers—they just needed someone to ask enough questions until they could talk through the answers they needed themselves. Greg sensed that Brent just needed to talk, so he started asking questions.

"What part of you wants to die?"

Brent struggled to express his thoughts. "I guess the part that has to deal with my parents' divorce and all the fighting. They're trying to do better, but Allison is still there and my mom still hates her. I just wish Allison would disappear and we could go back to being a family. I don't have much hope for that, though. All I can see is a continuation of all this."

Greg didn't have any answers, but Martin had assured him that was okay. "What part of you wants to live?"

"I guess the part that deep down believes God has answers for all this. I can't say I really believe it, but I want to. I'm *trying* to. There has to be some way of making sense of all this. And I guess there is a part of me that wants to know what my life will be like if I hang in there. I keep telling myself this can't last forever. Last Saturday I was just too tired to keep fighting it. But I want to now."

Brent lapsed into silence. His gentle breathing a few minutes later told Greg he was asleep. Greg rolled over to stare out the window at the falling snow and pray for his friend until he, too, fell asleep.

• • •

Kelly settled down on her window seat and drew her knees up close to give Julie room to join her. Once they were both settled, she reached down to the floor, grabbed the heavy blanket laying there, and pulled it up around her. Julie snuggled under her end, and then they sat in silence for several minutes and watched the snow.

"Snow is one of my most favorite things," Kelly said. "It's so peaceful, and it makes everything so beautiful. This will be my first white Christmas ever. I don't count the one we spent in Vermont skiing before Mom died. I was really young, but most importantly we weren't home. It didn't really feel like Christmas to me."

"This will be my first, too." Julie's voice became serious. "Kelly, I really appreciate you letting me spend the night. And thanks for listening to me so much lately. I just can't stand being alone right now." Julie's eyes filled with tears. "I know Brent's still alive, but I can't shake what might have been from my mind. And I still feel so guilty. I mean, I'm his girlfriend. I should have been able to help him."

Kelly sighed to herself. How long was Julie going to beat herself over the head for Brent's suicide attempt? She had told her friend over and over that it wasn't her fault, that Brent had made his own choices and decisions. Peggy had told Kelly she would just have to be patient and allow the Lord to help Julie work it out. Once more Kelly repeated the words she knew Julie needed to hear. She would do it as long as she needed to.

Suddenly Kelly had an urge to be out in the snow. She needed to let the wind blow her mind clear. She wanted to dance in the swirl of flakes.

"Let's go outside for a walk." Kelly stood up abruptly.

"Huh?"

"Let's go for a walk," she repeated. Already she was taking off her pajamas and pulling out other clothes.

"Are you nuts? It's almost midnight!" Julie's voice was mildly alarmed.

"Who cares? We can sleep late tomorrow. Your mom isn't picking you up until noon. Come on!"

Julie reluctantly kicked off the blanket. Grumbling, she began to pull off her pajamas. "I think you're nuts, but I'll do it."

Minutes later even Julie was having a good time in the winter wonderland. They had crept quietly down the stairs in order not to wake any of Kelly's family. Now they were crunching through snow down the middle of the street. The roads of the neighborhood lay like satiny white ribbons before them. This late at night no one else was out—no people to disturb the enveloping silence, no cars to mar the milky perfection of the snow. Street lights caught the flakes, turning them into a dancing light show that swirled and dipped in response to some unheard heavenly chorus. Trees and bushes bowed under their burdens as if admitting defeat to the storm. Sturdy balsams carried the snow as if they were holding up an offering to God.

Kelly and Julie walked in silence, absorbing the beauty of the night. Words were not necessary. Kelly sensed that Julie was finding peace as she viewed the evidence of God's majesty and control over his creation. Peggy had said it would take time—that God knew how to heal her hurt. Kelly was sure this was helping.

It was almost one when they rounded the last block and let themselves in the kitchen door. Kelly quietly fixed them cups of hot chocolate, grabbed some slabs of bread, and slipped upstairs. Minutes later, full and warm, they fell sound asleep.

THIRTEEN

I'll get it!" Emily ran through the den and opened the front door. "The Adamses are here!" she called out as she swung the door closed behind the family.

Seconds later, all six of them, Mr. and Mrs. Adams, Greg, and his three sisters, were in the kitchen. Kelly looked up from where she was putting the finishing touch on the fruit salad she had prepared for dinner and smiled. Peggy and her father welcomed their guests warmly and took everyone's coats. A second ringing of the doorbell produced Julie and her parents as well as Brent and his mom.

"Whew! I wasn't sure we were going to make it. My Volvo is not made for snow." Julie's father pulled off his coat as he spoke. "There are still some streets around town that aren't clear. Not having city snow equipment makes this clearing slow business. Thank goodness for the men who have tractors with blades. They're working hard, but it will take time."

The kitchen was getting very crowded, so Scott Marshall herded several people into the den where he had a huge fire roaring. Mrs. Adams, Mrs. Jackson, Julie, and her mom stayed behind to help finish preparing the meal. Peggy had decided it would be fun to have all the families join together for dinner before going to the Christmas Eve service at the church. Kelly knew that besides the time together being fun, Peggy and the other parents were trying to do all they could to support Brent and his mother.

It didn't take long to reheat the others' contributions and spread out a lavish buffet line in the kitchen. Kelly and Emily had set the tables in both the dining room and the kitchen. They just barely had room to squeeze in the fifteen of them. It was a good thing Kelly's grandparents couldn't come until the morning. She didn't know where they would have put them.

Scott Marshall led them all in a blessing, and then everyone grabbed a place in line. Peggy had provided a huge honey-baked Virginia ham that was so tender it was falling off the bone. Complementing the ham were fluffy sweet potatoes with a brown sugar and marshmallow glaze, corn pudding, spinach casserole, fruit salad, and puffy, homemade Parker House rolls just pulled from the oven. It was a meal fit for a king.

Greg laughed as he saw Brent surveying the food with wide eyes. "Maybe we should eat last so that everyone has a chance to get some."

"Maybe, but I'm not feeling that benevolent. I'm starving!" Brent made no move to relinquish his place of fourth in line.

Peggy laughed at Greg's comment. "There's plenty. You boys won't go away hungry, I promise. And I can guarantee the rest of us won't either."

Her words proved to be prophetic. Everyone had had their fill when they finally pushed back from the table.

"It's a good thing we have an hour and a half before the church service," laughed Brent's mom. "I couldn't stand and sing if I had to. I haven't eaten that much in ages."

Brent, from his chair in the kitchen, heard his mom's comment and leaned over to say to Greg, "That's no surprise. She hasn't cooked a real meal in a year and a half. Just me is not enough to get her to cook."

Greg frowned at the bitterness in his friend's voice. He knew it was going to take time for Brent to work through his anger. He was going to have to be patient. Comments like that weren't going to help, though. He exchanged a quiet glance with Kelly.

For the next hour the house rang with laughter as they divided up into teams and played charades. The whole game was angled toward Christmas— Christmas songs, movies, books, and traditions. Kelly's stomach hurt from laughing so hard, but she was having a great time. She loved having a house full of company. It made her home seem so alive.

Around eight Scott Marshall stood to speak. "If we're going to make it to the service, we better get going. We'll need extra time because of the roads. I'm glad y'all could come. This has been great!"

Amid a chorus of thank you's, everyone bundled up and headed out to their respective cars. The streets were still slick, so it was slow going, but they were at the church in plenty of time to get good seats.

Kelly drank in the beauty of the sanctuary of Kingsport Community Church as she and her family moved down the aisle. Two towering balsam trees, shipped in from the mountains, flanked both sides of the chancel area. Their only adornment were little white lights that seemed to dance and shimmer in the stillness of the building. The altar was graced with dozens of poinsettias reflecting the light of the advent candles and the dimly glowing chandelier. The only other illumination came from white candles glowing out into the night from the windows where they were perched. Keeping guard over the candles were lush green balsam wreaths bedecked with red, satin ribbons. Christmas music from the piano gently embraced each family as they found a place in a pew.

Kelly was glad to see that the Adams family was moving in to her row. If they all sat close, they could just fit. Sitting close was fine with Kelly. She smiled up at Greg as he came to stand beside her. He returned her smile and then reached down to take her hand. Glancing back, she saw Julie standing with her hand engulfed by Brent's. Julie looked the happiest she had been in several weeks.

The service was wonderful. Kelly loved all the traditional Christmas carols and there were very few they didn't sing that night. The music seemed to almost be a living thing as it swelled and soared through the building. When Pastor Stevens read the Christmas story from Luke, it became real to Kelly for the first time. That was *her* Lord he was talking about. Her Lord who loved her enough to come as a little baby and then grow up to die on a cross. She sat mesmerized, as if she had never heard it before. To close the service, everyone lit the small candle they had received on their way in. The place glowed with what to Kelly was a heavenly light. Glancing back, she saw a peace on Brent's face that she hadn't seen for a long time. He noticed her glance and gave her a warm smile. Julie's smile was radiant as well.

This was going to be a good Christmas, Kelly thought. What could possibly go wrong now?

• • •

Greg dropped his family off and then headed toward Kelly's house. They had arranged to have some time alone to exchange Christmas gifts. It was almost eleven when they arrived. Her father was just checking the doors and lights before heading to bed.

"Merry Christmas Eve, Greg," he said with a smile. "I'll see you tomorrow for the party."

"Thanks, Mr. Marshall. Merry Christmas Eve to you, too. See you tomorrow."

Peggy and Emily had already gone to bed, so Greg and Kelly had the den to themselves. Greg picked up another small log to add to the fire. Kelly moved a couple of the floor pillows closer to the flame, and they sank down on them. Both were content to stare into the flames and think.

Finally, Greg reached into his pocket and pulled out a small box.

"Merry Christmas, Kelly."

Heart pounding, Kelly took the small box and carefully unwrapped it. She gasped when she raised the hinged lid. Gleaming up at her was a delicate gold cross on a golden chain.

"I wanted you to have something that reminded you both of me and of who holds our lives and relationship together." Greg took it and very carefully put it around her neck.

Kelly's words were only a whisper. "Thank you, Greg. It's beautiful. It's the best present I've ever gotten." She sat silent for a minute, overwhelmed by the idea that Greg Adams was her boyfriend. Then she stood and moved over to the Christmas tree. Reaching underneath, she pulled out a large, flat package.

Taking it from her, Greg pulled the paper off. His immediate response was a low whistle and a grin. "Kelly, this is awesome. Thank you!" It was obvious he liked it.

Kelly was relieved. She had put a lot of work into her gift, but she wasn't sure what Greg would think of it. She had made a collage of pictures. The large, center picture was one Peggy had taken of the two of them when they were unaware. They were both laughing and looking into the other's eyes. Kelly had surrounded it with pictures of Shandy, Crystal, the two of them riding, her teaching. There was even one she had snapped when Greg was swinging in the barn. At the top of the matting she had carefully drawn a cross to signify the Lordship of Christ over their relationship. She had also included the picture of her laughing from Santa's lap.

Greg pored over each picture. When he finally looked up, she was thrilled by the expression in his eyes. She was sure he was going to kiss her. Instead, he took her hands and asked, "Can we pray together? I want to thank God for our friendship and pray that nothing ever happens to mess it up. All this stuff with Brent reminded me how temporary friendships can be."

Kelly nodded. Would this guy ever cease to surprise her? Bowing her head they prayed for several minutes. When she raised her head, he was staring into her eyes. Rising abruptly he pulled her to her feet.

"It's time for me to go. Christmas morning starts early around my house."

A little confused, Kelly followed him through the kitchen to the back door. Only then did he turn and give her a gentle kiss.

"I couldn't kiss you in there, Kelly. The fire and the pillows might have made it a little too tempting. I mean it when I say I don't want to do anything to mess up our friendship. Good night. I'll see you tomorrow." With those words, Greg opened the door and slipped out into the frigid night.

Kelly simply stared after him. Watching him drive down the street, she finally closed the door to the wintry night. She gave herself the luxury of sinking down next to the fire and reliving the magic of the night. The soft glow of the Christmas tree mingling with the crackle and flames of the fire wrapped her in a blanket of warm feelings. When she felt her eyes getting heavy, she carefully closed the glass doors on the fireplace and went to bed. She was holding her cross in her hand when she drifted off to sleep.

• • •

Kelly turned her father's four-wheel-drive truck into the gate at Porter's Stables. Rolling down the window, she gave the familiar call to her filly. Then she sat back and watched. Her filly racing across the pasture was always a beautiful sight, but her black beauty against the snowy white of the pasture was breathtaking. Shandy's buckskin body matched Crystal's stride for stride as they moved in unison. The clouds of snow kicked up by their flying hooves seemed to hang suspended in the cold air before drifting back to fill in the marred landscape. The clouds had cleared during the morning, and now the sky was crystal blue with an occasional fluffy cloud. Pressing the accelerator, Kelly drove to meet her filly.

She had just put both of the horses in their stalls when Greg joined her. Kelly looked at her watch. It was four. They only had an hour before they needed to head to her house to finish getting ready for the Happy Birthday, Jesus party tonight.

"Merry Christmas, Kelly!"

"Merry Christmas yourself! How's your day been?"

"It's been great! Brent and his mom just left. He'll be at your house for the party later. They seemed to have a good time, and he looked really happy. He told me before he left that it's the best Christmas he's had in years."

"I'm so glad. I've had a good day, too. My grandparents came in early this morning. We waited for them to have breakfast, and then we opened all the gifts. The neatest part, though, was Dad reading the Christmas story again around the breakfast table. Then we all went around and each one of us had to give the family a gift. It was cool. My dad's gift to us was to give both Emily and I our own nights out with him once every two weeks. My gift was to teach both Emily and Peggy how to ride this spring when it gets warmer."

Greg grinned. "What a neat idea!"

"Yeah. Someone told Dad about it, so he decided to do it. Then we went in and opened our gifts. I got some neat stuff but nothing I like so much as my cross."

"I know what you mean. I have your collage standing on my desk so I can see it all the time."

They smiled at each other, and then laughed as Crystal and Shandy demanded attention by stomping their feet and snorting.

"Okay, Crystal, okay!" Kelly said. "Someone must have clued you in that it's Christmas. I just happen to have a special treat for you." Crystal very seldom got sweet feed, but today was special.

Kelly and Greg had mixed up a special blend of sweet feed and bran. Pulling out the thermos full of hot water she had brought with her, Kelly took the bucket Greg handed her and poured the mixture in. Greg was busy chopping up the carrots and apples he had brought along. He dumped them in, and Kelly poured a small amount of hot water over the concoction. She gave a quick stir and then dumped half the mixture in Crystal's feed bin and gave the remainder to Shandy. Their happy munching and slurping convinced Kelly and Greg their Christmas present was a hit.

They spent the remainder of their time grooming their horses and then turned them back out in the pasture. Mandy would be home to bring Crystal and Shandy in soon, but they could play in the snow until then. They seemed to agree with the idea. As soon as they were turned loose, they lifted their heads and tails high and took off across the field.

● ● ●

By the time Kelly said goodbye to her last guest, she was convinced the night had been a success. Twenty of her and Greg's friends had shown up from youth group—Brent and Julie included—for the Happy Birthday, Jesus party. They had had a special time of singing and praying together. Kelly was glad she had taken time to just focus on Jesus— to be reminded that he was the reason they had this month-long celebration. Julie had surprised them by bringing a cake with "Happy Birthday, Jesus" inscribed on it.

When Kelly crawled into bed that night, she allowed her mind to wander back on all that had happened that month. Things would probably be getting back to normal now, she thought sleepily. The ski trip would be a lot of fun, but she couldn't imagine anything especially exciting occurring.

FOURTEEN

By nine the following morning the Adamses, who had picked up Julie and Brent on the way, were knocking at Kelly's back door. Greg's parents were each driving one of the twelve-passenger vans they had rented for their trip. In twenty minutes they had finished loading the vans with clothing, gear, and massive quantities of food.

"It looks like we're leaving for a month, not for five days. If this van could groan in protest at all the weight, I think it would." Scott Marshall laughed as he crammed the last bag in and pulled the door shut.

Emily jumped up and down with excitement. They were going to stop and pick up her best friend, Shannon. The whole group seemed to vibrate with anticipation. Greg's father had announced that the ski conditions were perfect, both on the trails and on the parkway. The cold weather was supposed to stick, and they were even forecasting more flurries for later in the week. Deposits had already been made on the cross-country skis. They were going to stop on the way up the mountain to have everyone fitted. Racks were on both vans, ready to carry them.

There were a few minutes of chaos while decisions were made about who would ride where. The end result was Kelly, Greg, Julie, and Brent riding in the blue van. Emily and Shannon would join Greg's mom and dad and three sisters. Everyone was happy with the arrangement. In minutes they were pulling out of the drive and heading toward the mountains surrounding Asheville.

In only two and a half hours, with two pit stops along the way, they arrived at the parking lot of the Alpine Ski Center. It took more than an hour for everyone to have their skis and boots fitted. Greg and Brent were placing them on the racks as they were selected. Kelly and Julie, along with the rest of the crew, opted to enjoy the crackling fire radiating from the fireplace in the cozy lounge area that was part of the store. Ski magazines were in abundant supply, and a huge container of hot water kept them supplied with instant coffee, tea, and hot chocolate.

"What if I make an absolute fool of myself?" Julie was looking at a full-page picture in a magazine as she wailed out the words.

Kelly glanced over and laughed. "Trust me. We won't be hitting major downhill slopes, and you aren't competing with the world champion you're staring at. We're just going up to have a good time. Most of our trails will be flat or have easy slopes."

"But I've never done this before. And you're great at it!"

"I'd hardly call myself great. I've been skiing for years, but they're usually just short trips. In the last three years, we haven't had enough snow to even come."

Julie looked puzzled. "I thought ski resorts had snow machines so they could make their own snow."

"They do, but that's for downhill skiing. There are a lot of cross-country skiers who are taking their skis on the downhill slopes now—they call it Nordic downhill—but Dad and I enjoy the old classical style. We just head out into the woods on trails, so if God isn't sending snow, there just isn't any."

"That's a pain."

Kelly smiled. "Maybe, but I like it better that way. I'm not into crowds, and I hate waiting for the lines at the chair lifts. I also hate dodging people and hoping I don't run over someone who just fell in front of me. I like being out in the open woods, able to go anywhere I want to. It's so quiet and free. Cross-country skiing is definitely for me." Kelly paused and then laughed. "Of course, if I had the chance to head out to the west where the ski runs sometimes take an hour to ski, I wouldn't turn my nose up at it. There aren't any ski resorts like that around here, though. Cross-country is my love."

Julie nodded thoughtfully. "I see what you mean. It sounds like a lot of fun. I just hope I can do it. I don't want to look stupid."

Peggy overheard their conversation and spoke up. "You'll do fine, Julie. If I can do it, you can. I just learned how last year when I visited a friend in Vermont before Scott and I got married. She kept telling me it was like walking. It is kind of, even though it's more than that. It may take a while before you're gliding along gracefully, but you'll pick it up."

Just then Scott walked up. "We're out of here, gang!" he announced. "Emily and Shannon just got their equipment, so we're set to go. Another forty-five minutes and we'll be there. I know everyone is hungry. Can we wait until we get there, or do we need to stop and eat?"

Peggy looked around for reactions and then suggested, "I think we should keep going. We can fix quick sandwiches when we get there. I don't want to miss any more daylight and ski time."

"Yeah!" Kelly and Julie cheered as they headed out to the vans. Brent and Greg finished strapping down the skis and jumped in.

Forty-five minutes later they were turning up the drive to the log cabin the Adamses and the Marshalls had rented. The next half-hour was a flurry of activity as bags, gear, and food were brought in. Only then did Kelly take the time to inspect her surroundings. Their home for the next five days was open and spacious. The downstairs was one huge living area with thick carpet and big, comfortable sofas and chairs. A huge bearskin rug dominated the area in front of the natural stone fireplace. A counter separated the kitchen from the rest of the area, but it was all open as well. Huge bay windows, looking out over the snow-covered valley below, completed the side of the house graced by the fireplace. There was no television but close inspection of a large cedar chest revealed a treasure of games and books. A huge picnic table served as the dining facility. Bar stools at the counter would seat the spillover of their group.

"Hey! Come check out upstairs!"

Julie and Kelly ran upstairs in response to Greg's call. They found five huge bedrooms with two bathrooms along the hall and a bigger one in the master suite. Kelly and Julie would have their own room; Greg and Brent would share one; both sets of parents would have their own room; and the five younger girls would slumber party it in the room with two sets of bunks and a roll-away bed.

"So, Dad. Who's going to get the room with the jacuzzi in the bathroom? If y'all can't decide, Brent and I will be happy to take care of the problem and stay in there."

Mr. Adams laughed. "Good try, but you don't stand a chance. We're taking care of that decision in a very democratic way. We're going to flip for it!" Producing a coin from his pocket, he turned to Scott. "Do you want to flip or call?"

"Call. Heads."

"Tails!" Mr. Adams said with a grin. "We'll let you know how the jacuzzi is. If you're on good behavior, we might even let you use it."

Scott and Peggy laughed good-naturedly as they carried their gear up to their bedroom.

It only took twenty minutes to lay out sandwich fixings and prepare lunch. Everyone helped themselves. Paper plates and cups made cleanup quick and easy.

"It's three. We have a couple of hours of light yet. I say we go out on the golf course that's nearby and get everyone used to their skis, give lessons—all that kind of stuff. Do I have takers?" Scott Marshall looked around the room as he spoke.

The immediate response was cheers.

"Okay, then. Go get your gear on. Remember, several light layers are best. Save the heavy coats for tubing and sledding. You burn a lot of energy when you're skiing, and you don't want to get too hot."

The whole group scattered to follow his instructions. All but Peggy and Sherri Adams.

"Sherri and I are going to stay behind to get dinner started," Peggy explained. "We'll follow you once we have it ready to slip in the oven. It shouldn't take us long, but we'd rather do it now than when we're tired and hungry."

In fifteen minutes the whole group was assembled at the front door. A short five-minute drive landed them at the Pisgah Valley Golf Course. Other people had the same idea, but it wasn't crowded. Grabbing their poles and skis, all eleven of them were soon headed down to the fairway on hole nine. It was the only one not occupied. Brent, Greg, and Mr. Adams immediately took off down the fairway in search of some hills. All three were experienced skiers. Kelly, who had opted to stay behind with Julie, pressed down feelings of envy. She knew Julie would feel much more confident with her support, and there was going to be plenty of time to ski once Julie became comfortable. She lined up with Julie, Emily, Shannon, and Greg's three younger sisters. Emily had last skied when she was seven and had only skied for a couple of days then. She was a beginner as well.

Scott smiled at his entourage and began his instructions. "Anyone who can walk can cross-country ski, but you don't want to end up walking on your skis! In order to ski well and really enjoy it, you need to learn how to glide on your skis and let them work for you. That's when it becomes fun." Reaching over, he picked up his skis and showed everyone how to clamp the toe ends of their boots into the bindings. Once everyone was standing, he showed them how to grip their poles, making sure the cloth loops at the handles were securely around their wrists. Checking everyone, he glided around to stand in front of them.

As he did so, Peggy and Sherri drove into the parking lot. Noticing them, Scott excused himself and skied over to where they were getting their gear on. Moments later he returned. "Peggy and Sherri are going to head down the course on their own. I told them too many teachers could mess up the process. They didn't seem to mind too much." The group laughed, and then Scott continued his lesson.

"There are three basic types of cross-country— classical skiing, freestyle skiing, and Nordic downhill. We're going to concentrate on classical skiing. I've played around with the others and they're great fun, but for beginners I think this is the way to go. You'll feel most secure this way."

Kelly's father proceeded to demonstrate the skill of gliding on one ski. "Gliding on one ski is really important to learn because the longer you can glide on each ski, the easier you move across the snow. You may shuffle for a while until you feel comfortable, but you'll get the hang of it." Everyone laughed as he exaggerated a shuffle across the snow. "While you're practicing this, try and stay on one ski for as long as possible. You'll probably find one leg is stronger than the other, but try not to baby the weaker leg. See how long you can hold the other ski off the ground. And don't be afraid to fall. That's part of learning. You'll get the hang of it."

The late afternoon air rang with laughter and groans of frustration as the six girls labored to get the feel of their skis. Kelly laughed along with them as she offered encouragement and tips. She was thrilled to see Julie catch on very quickly. She smiled at the look of excitement on her friend's face.

"I told you this was no big deal."

Julie laughed. "Well, this part anyway. What's next?"

Scott overheard her and laughed. "Ready for lesson number two already, are you?" Glancing around, he noticed that everyone seemed to have gotten the hang of it. The younger girls weren't gliding very far, but at least they were gliding. Calling them over, he said, "Now we figure out how to move from ski to ski so you can get somewhere. What that really means is that you need to be able to transfer your weight between skis. Your goal is to transfer your weight crisply so that only one ski remains on the snow at a time. If you can't do that, you'll be locked into the good ol' snow shuffle."

He demonstrated what he was talking about, and then he and Kelly once again offered encouragement and tips. At one point, Kelly looked over and returned the warm grin her father gave her. It was fun to be working with him like this. She was glad she had stayed behind. She could ski with the boys later.

An hour passed before Brent, Greg, and Mr. Adams skied back up, flushed and exuberant. By then, all of Scott's students were moving easily across the snow on their skis. There would be a lot of practice needed to improve their style, but they had the basics down. Julie was glowing as Brent skied up to her.

"I can do it, Brent! This is really fun."

"I knew you'd catch on quick. Why don't we make a quick run down to the end of the fairway on hole eleven? It's pretty flat."

Kelly glanced at her watch and then over at her dad. He nodded his head. "We have a few minutes before we have to leave. Peggy and Sherri said they would be back at five-thirty. That gives you twenty minutes. Have fun."

Kelly felt a surge of adrenalin as she pushed off on her skis and glided smoothly across the snow. Looking back, she saw Brent with Julie, so she felt okay about taking off. Seconds later, Greg glided up next to her. Side by side they flew across the snow, laughing as they strove to see who could edge into the lead. Kelly was sure Greg could beat her, but he was content to stay even. The setting sun had turned the sky into a palette of brilliant pinks and purples. Its reflection on the snow made Kelly's heart catch with the beauty of it. Too soon they had come to the end of the fairway. Turning around, they met Julie and Brent. Knowing it was time to head back, they slowed their pace and skied with their two friends. Julie was becoming more and more confident. By the time they got back to the car, she was doing really well.

"I can't wait to hit the trails tomorrow," Julie cried.

"You sure don't sound like the girl in the ski shop this morning," Peggy teased.

"I just never knew it was so easy. This is great. I thought I would just be figuring out how to stand up by the end of the week!"

Everyone laughed and piled into the vans.

• • •

Peggy had divided the group into two dinner teams. Working together, it didn't take long to finish preparing the meal. The two large casserole dishes were licked clean of any remnants of spaghetti. Three large loaves of bread were demolished and the huge bowl of salad was empty.

"I was afraid we had brought too much food. Now I'm wondering if we have enough! We may be making some store runs," laughed Sherri. "At least we know they like the food."

After dinner, Emily and Shannon picked out some games that the younger girls were quickly into. Kelly was content to slug out in front of the fireplace with her three friends on the bearskin rug. The adults were comfortably snuggled on the sofas. The only movement for an hour was Greg's reaching over to add more wood to the fire.

Finally, Kelly roused herself and talked adults and kids alike into a loud game of Taboo. Laughter and shouting rang through the house as the females battled the guys for dominance. When it was all over, the guys had edged out the girls by just two points.

"You girls might have beat us in Pictionary, but I warned you we would be back for revenge." Brent scowled and beat his hands against his chest.

Kelly turned her nose up in the air. "We have to let you guys beat us *sometime*. If we had beaten the four of you, there would have been no living with you. The male ego can only take so much humiliation, you know. We were trying to be kind."

Greg just laughed at her. "You've never *let* anyone win in your life, Kelly. It's not in your blood. Just admit you lost, fair and square."

Kelly laughed along with him. "Oh, all right! But we'll be back, and next time you'll regret you ever gave us another chance."

"Okay, truce, everyone!" Peggy grinned and held up her hands. "How about some dessert?"

While everyone was eating, Greg noticed that Brent had a very pensive look about him. He didn't look depressed, just kind of sad. What was going on? Greg knew that talking was the best thing. He was also learning how to press through and get his friend to communicate. Finishing off his cake, he stood. "Hey Brent, let's go out on the porch for a few minutes. I'd like to look at the lights in the valley."

Brent looked up in surprise, but agreed. "Okay. Let me get my coat."

Minutes later, he and Brent were standing outside, leaning against the railing, taking in deep breaths of the delicious mountain air.

"Feels like snow," Brent commented.

"Yeah. The weatherman said we might get more." Silence fell for a few moments and then Greg asked, "What are you thinking about?"

Brent looked at him and gave a small grin. "That seems to have become your favorite question lately."

Greg just nodded.

Brent stared down at the valley and then began to talk. "I guess I'm just jealous."

"Jealous?"

"Yeah. You and Kelly have such great families. So does Julie. I really wish mine could be that way. I love being up here with you guys, but it sure points out how lousy my family is. I wish it was different, that's all."

Greg thought about his friend's words. "You know, I was wondering the other day how I would feel if I had a family like yours. It would be hard, that's for sure. I don't know why it has to be that way, but I've thought a lot about what Martin talked about the night we went sledding. I don't think your dad leaving is a good thing, but I have to believe God can bring good out of it. It might take a while, but I think he can."

"I'm trying to believe that," Brent sighed. "Sometimes God seems really close, and then other times it feels like he's a million miles away. I'm trying to trust him, but it sure is hard. There is a good thing about being here, though. It's pretty cool to see that all families don't have trouble. You don't often hear a lot about families that love each other and have fun together."

"Yeah."

Silence fell between them as Greg prayed that God would make himself very real to his friend. He wondered what it would take for God to answer that prayer in Brent's life.

FIFTEEN

Kelly woke early the next morning. Reaching over, she shook Julie's shoulders, jumped from the bed, and raced to the window. "Look! It's snowing again. Yahoo! Look at it come down!" Turning, she saw Julie bury her head under the covers again. "Hey, you! Get up. I don't want to miss any skiing. You are *not* allowed to be lazy on this trip. We didn't come up here to sleep."

Julie groaned and threw the covers back. "Do you *have* to be so cheerful—and loud? Whatever happened to waking up slowly and quietly?"

"Boring!" Kelly's one word said it all as she tossed a pillow at her friend and opened the bedroom door. "I'm going to wake the boys up."

"Too late." Greg appeared from nowhere and shoved a handful of snow down the back of Kelly's shirt. The two boys had obviously been up for a while, enjoying the fresh snowfall.

Kelly's shriek filled the whole house. "You... you...bum!" Wrenching away, she twisted free from his hold.

Julie laughed at her until she saw Brent advancing down the hall. Jumping up, she pulled Kelly back into the safety of their room. Slamming the door, she locked it. The two girls collapsed on the bed laughing.

The whole house was awake after that. There was no way they could have slept through Kelly's shriek. The girls heard the adults laughing as Greg admitted his prank. It was going to be a fun day.

Breakfast was delayed while everyone ran out to play in the falling snow. Kelly and Julie were on breakfast crew, so when Mrs. Adams called, they shook off the snow and ran in to help with the steaming pot of oatmeal simmering on the stove. Quickly they put out fresh sticks of butter, a big bowl of brown sugar, a pitcher of cream, and a can of ground cinnamon. A gallon of milk, two loaves of homemade bread, strawberry preserves, glasses, bowls, and spoons finished off the spread. Their call brought everyone running.

"Yum! Oatmeal!" Emily exclaimed. "This is a great meal for a snowy day." Her bright eyes were as excited as her voice, and red spots shone on her cheeks. Shannon looked just as happy.

"It will stay with you. And on a day like today, that's pretty important. Your body will be burning up a lot of energy," Eric Adams said as he dug into the huge bowl he had just scooped up.

• • •

The Blue Ridge Parkway was their destination for the day. Kelly loved this part of North Carolina and was looking forward to sharing it with Greg. The ribbon of highway that stretched along the Blue Ridge Mountains from Front Royal, Virginia—where it was named Skyline Drive—575 miles to Cherokee, North Carolina, in the southwest corner of the state made up the Blue Ridge Parkway. It was 575 miles of unending beauty, with everything from huge meadows, towering mountains, sheer rock faces, plunging waterfalls, and stone formations. In the spring it was covered with wildly blooming rhododendron and mountain laurel. Summer brought an abundance of wildflowers and blueberries. Fall called people from all over the country to delight in its riotous colors as the ridge prepared for winter. Winter could be brutal but beautiful. Long stretches of the parkway were closed to all but hikers and cross-country skiers.

The guy at the Alpine ski store had told them of a skiing stretch that had a relatively easy grade before changing in elevation and becoming a grueling climb. The five-mile section, ten miles round-trip, would be plenty for one day.

By ten, everyone was unloading gear from the vans and unstrapping skis from the racks. Peggy volunteered to stay back with the younger girls who couldn't keep the same pace as the other skiers. The faster skiers agreed to carry the gear and have lunch all ready when the others caught up with them.

Greg and Brent grinned at each other in anticipation. They had laid awake until late last night, as Brent told Greg stories about the biking and hiking he had done with his father on the Blue Ridge Parkway. That had been when Brent was younger and his family was still together. It had been good to remember some happy times, Brent had said. He realized how easy it was to forget the good times when things got hard.

Julie used the few minutes while everyone was getting ready to glide around a little bit and remember all she had learned the day before.

"You'll be a pro by the end of the day, Julie. Practice makes better, and you'll have plenty of that today," Kelly encouraged.

"I hope you're right. I don't want to slow the group down. Are you sure I shouldn't stay behind?"

"Absolutely. We're sticking together. You'll be fine. And it's not like we're out to set records or something."

"Let's go, team." Scott's words were the signal his group was waiting for.

With a yell, the seven of them pushed off and headed down the satiny ribbon stretching into the distance. The snow had tapered off to a gentle flurry, so the visibility was good. The snow on the parkway was deep, but lots of ski traffic had kept it fairly packed. The two inches they had picked up that morning gave it a nice topping. The group was able to glide smoothly along, laughing and talking as they passed rock faces frozen into glistening ice formations and trees struggling hard to carry their load of snow.

Once they started up the gradual incline facing them, the laughing and talking tapered off. Instead, everyone concentrated on breathing and making every glide efficient. Julie was thankful she had Brent's tracks to follow in. She knew that following someone was much easier than breaking the initial tracks. Brent's excellent condition was obvious as he plowed ahead. His near brush with death seemed to be far behind him.

"How about a break?"

Kelly groaned in thankfulness at her father's words. How had he known she was dying of thirst? And hot. In spite of the cold, the exercise was causing her to sweat. Gliding to a standstill, she released her bindings, stepped off her skis, and sat down on a nearby boulder. Shrugging her daypack from her shoulders, she reached in for her water bottle and began to drink.

"Everyone needs to follow Kelly's example," her father spoke to all of them. "Drink plenty of water. It helps your body regulate its temperature. You may think just because it's cold that you don't need to drink. That's wrong, especially as much as you're sweating and burning up energy. If you wait till you're thirsty, you've waited too long. Your body requires at least a gallon a day when you're out like this. That's why I had everyone tank up before we left. That's also why there is a big cooler of water back in the van. You'll handle the cold and exercise a lot better if you drink plenty." Pausing, he lifted his water bottle to follow his own advice. Then he continued, "You might also want to take off a layer when we get started again. It's better to have one to put back on when you begin to cool off. We'll be stopping awhile for lunch, and I don't want anyone to get too cold."

"You sure know a lot about this cold weather stuff, Mr. Marshall," Brent said with admiration.

"I should. I grew up in the woods of Minnesota. That's *winter* up there! My dad taught me about cold weather survival when I was still just a kid. He wouldn't let me go out alone in the woods until I knew how to take care of myself."

"I sure would like to learn that stuff. My dad and I have always been up here in warm, or just cool, weather."

"You're welcome to pick my brain while we're here," Mr. Marshall grinned. "I also have a pack full of emergency gear in case anyone wants to head out for a while. I'm carrying it now. That's why mine is so much bigger than y'alls. I'll explain it to you, if you'd like. Maybe at lunch."

"That would be great, Mr. Marshall. Thanks!" Brent's smile lit his face.

Greg was satisfied his friend was having a good time and that any thoughts of suicide were far from his mind.

• • •

One hour later the lead group located the perfect spot for lunch. Skiing off the road, they entered the huge meadow overlook. The snow had stopped and the sky had cleared. Glistening mountain peaks stretched as far as the eye could see. Fluffy clouds dipped and swirled around the tops, trying to compete with the whiteness of the snow. Finding a large boulder to shelter them from the wind, they discovered the sun made the area a very comfortable place to relax.

Peggy and the girls skied in to join them thirty minutes later. The morning's jaunt had greatly improved all of their skills. They were starving and the faster group was ready for them. They had pulled out slabs of bread, slices of cheddar cheese, and plenty of apples, grapes, and oranges. The hungry crew fell on the feast and demolished every crumb and morsel.

"Where's dessert?" Emily asked.

"You can have sugar when you get home tonight," her father answered. "You don't need it out here. Sugar gives you an initial rush, but then it slows you down and makes you more tired. Complex carbohydrates and protein are best when you're out like this. They're the best energy foods."

"Hey, Mr. Marshall," Brent said. "Do you think we could talk about the cold weather survival stuff now? I'd really like to see what you have in your pack."

"You bet. You're really into the outdoors, aren't you?"

"Yeah. I'd rather be outside than anywhere. I've always wanted to go winter camping but never had the chance."

Scott Marshall reached behind him and picked up his pack. "You never know when you'll get caught by cold weather and not be able to get back to shelter. Cold weather can kill people, if they aren't prepared." Opening the pack, he came to the first thing and pulled it out. "I always have a first aid kit with me." He showed Brent everything it contained. "I made this one myself because the prepacked ones are usually missing a few things I think are important. When I pack my kit, I am primarily thinking about cuts, sprains, breaks—that kind of thing. I'm also prepared with painkillers and antacids. Besides that, I always carry water purification drops. They don't make the water taste great, but if you're stuck somewhere you don't want to have to worry about the water making you sick."

Brent nodded, intent on every word.

Scott reached in and pulled out more items. "I always carry a whistle. You never know when you'll get lost and need to summon help. Your voice can give out after a while. Besides, a whistle will carry a lot longer way than your voice. I also have a good supply of waterproof and windproof matches. I think you can figure out why that's important. Another essential item are these fire starters. I make them at home by rolling newspaper tightly together, tying it with string, and then soaking it in paraffin. If you're trying to get wet wood to light, they're invaluable."

He pulled out some more items. "I carry several of these reflective 'space blankets.' They do a great job of holding in body heat and keeping you warm. I usually stick in a few plastic bags which help keep you dry and also hold in heat. I always have a compass, but it's only handy if you know how to read it. A knife can be your best friend. Another essential part of the pack is a flashlight with several fresh batteries. Darkness can defeat you quickly, so a source of light is very important. Oh, and cord. I almost forgot it was in here. It can be a great help in fixing a shelter if you find yourself in a bind."

He finished pulling out things and stopped to think. "I've already told you how important water is. Food is just as important. It's much better to eat several small meals to keep your energy constant than to eat a couple of big meals. I always take more than I think I'm going to need. Other than that..." Scott stared off into space a moment. "Always tell people where you are going—at least a general direction. If you don't come out, people need to have some idea of where to start looking." Smiling at Brent, he began to stuff things back in the bag.

"What about clothing?" Brent asked. "What's the best stuff to wear?"

"Well, I'd start out with long johns. I like the kind made out of polypropylene. They draw moisture away from the body without getting soaked and dry quickly themselves. They also do a good job of keeping you warm even if they're wet. I'd top that with wool because, again, it will keep you warm even if you get wet. Keep in mind I'm talking about cross-country ski wear. You don't really want a heavy jacket because it will get too hot. I would top a wool sweater with a waterproof, light-weight jacket that fits easily in your pack if you get too warm. Wind pants can come in handy, too, if you're going someplace really cold. Besides that, I'd take warm gloves and a hat with a face mask. You never know when you'll need it." Scott took a deep breath and grinned at Brent. "You can't possibly hold any more information for now. And we need to head back before everyone completely falls asleep out here."

The downhill trip to the van was exciting. Kelly sang at the top of her lungs as she centered over her skis and flew down the hill. What had taken them two hours to climb only took thirty minutes to descend. Julie's face was flushed with the cold when

she joined Kelly by the van, but her eyes were glowing with delight.

"I'm so glad Brent and I got to join you guys. I
never knew skiing could be this much fun. I'm having a blast! I see what you mean now about feeling so
free and open. No lines, no crowds, just us and the
mountains."

Kelly grinned at her friend. "You got it. I can tell
you're as hooked as me. Horseback riding will always
be my favorite thing to do, but I think skiing follows
a close second."

• • •

The next two days were a haze of skiing, tubing,
and sledding. The four friends enjoyed skiing the
most. Using a map Scott Marshall had provided,
they spent hours exploring trails in the local mountains. Julie became as proficient as the other three.
Whether sidestepping up the steepest hills or whiz-
zing down the other side, they were intent on having
fun. And they did. They picnicked with sparkling
cider and skied one night on the golf course under a
glowing moon. Kelly's favorite discovery had been a
cascading waterfall. All around the face and the
base of the fall were huge ice formations created by
the spray from the water. She had stared at it for a
half-hour before the others had convinced her to
move on.

They also held a a snow-sculpting contest in the
front yard. There were several snowmen, a huge
turtle created by Julie, a large soccer ball crafted by
Brent, and Kelly's rendition of a horse head. They

had great fun posing by their works of art while Peggy and Sherri took pictures.

Except for the one moonlight run on the golf course, the nights were a time for relaxation and games. There had been no more snow after the first night, so each day was clear and cold. When evening arrived, there was not enough energy to do more than eat and lounge around. The constantly blazing fire added charm and coziness to the family room.

"Hey, Dad, have you got any good ideas for our final run in the morning? We want to go someplace special."

Scott Marshall thought carefully before he answered. Reaching behind him, he pulled out a map from the bookshelf. Spreading it out, he motioned Kelly and the other three over. "If I were you, I would head to Champion Trail. It does a ten-mile loop around one of the mountains. You'll catch some awesome vistas as well as beautiful wooded areas and a couple of waterfalls."

Kelly's eyes lit up at the mention of waterfalls.

Greg laughed when he saw her expression. "Looks like we have our trail."

All of them listened carefully as Mr. Marshall told them how to get there. It was only five miles from the cabin in the van. They would leave early the next morning and be back by two in the afternoon. That would give them plenty of time to pack up and get home and rested for the New Year's Eve service at church.

With their decision made, the four decided to call it a night so they could get up in the morning. As they headed upstairs, the rest of the group decided to call it a night as well. The radio, usually turned on to catch the next day's weather conditions, remained silent.

S I X T E E N

Greg rolled over as his watch alarm went off at seven. *Funny,* he thought, *it should be light outside.* Crawling out of bed, he noted the cloudy conditions that were causing the lingering darkness. They'd better get going. Shaking Brent awake, he padded down the hall to knock softly on the girls' door. A soft reply from Julie assured him the girls were awake.

Fifteen minutes later all four of them were surrounding the kitchen counter as Kelly and Julie made huge bowls of oatmeal and Greg and Brent packed lunch.

Kelly looked over and laughed. "We're not going out for a week. It's only lunch, you know."

Greg smiled but continued to pack his bag with bread, fruit, cheese, cookies, sandwich meats, and carrot sticks. "We're growing boys. I'd rather bring some back than be hungry. This is our last run. I want to make the most of it."

Brent headed into the storeroom to grab Scott Marshall's pack. Ever since his talk with Kelly's dad, he had carried it with him whenever they went out.

195

"You sure you want to carry that thing, Brent?" Julie asked. "Doesn't it get awfully heavy? We're just going for a loop around the mountain. Why don't you leave it behind this time?"

"Nothing doing," Brent replied firmly. "Where I go, it goes."

Julie shrugged her shoulders. "Just trying to make your life easier."

Breakfast eaten and all their gear packed, they were ready to leave. Brent looked up at the heavy sky. "Anyone listen to the weather?" Everyone shook their heads. "Do you think we should?"

Greg looked at his watch. "It doesn't come on for another fifteen minutes at eight. Do you want to wait?"

"Why don't we listen for it on the radio in the van?" Julie suggested.

Kelly shook her head. "We can't. The radio doesn't work in the blue van." She thought a moment. "I say let's get going. This is our last trip and I don't want to miss any of it."

"I don't know," Brent said, his voice tinged with concern. "Maybe we should wait."

"Oh, come on!" Kelly playfully dragged him toward the door. "The weather is going to be fine!"

The radio in the cabin was playing softly when they left. As the van reached the bottom of the road, an announcer came on:

> *Just in from the National Weather Service. There is a major winter storm approaching our area. Radar indicates it will hit between noon and one. This is a major winter storm.*

*You are advised against travel. Stay in, if at
all possible.*

The rest of the cabin continued to sleep peacefully.

• • •

Greg led the way up the trail after everyone had
put their skis on. The first two miles were a gentle
grade that provided just the warmup they needed
before the trail began to climb.

"My dad was right. This is beautiful!" Kelly's
voice was hushed as they glided along beneath huge
stands of fir and spruce. There was at least three feet
of snow on the ground, but the trail had been packed
down by snowmobiles. Kelly was thankful the snowmobiles had been there but was glad they weren't
now. She would have hated for the quiet and beauty
to be marred by the loud roaring motors. She felt as
if she and her friends were in their own little world.
The only sound was the swishing of their skis and
the awakening songs of the winter birds.

As the trail began to climb, the woods were dominated by oaks and poplar. Their naked limbs con-
trasted sharply with the heavy, gray sky. Every now
and then, Kelly saw Brent study the sky.

"Is something wrong, Brent?"

He turned concerned eyes to her but laughed it
off. "Oh, I was just thinking that I'd hate to get
caught up here in a snowstorm. We don't know the
area very well."

Greg laughed at his words. "You've been letting
Kelly's dad get to you. Relax. We'll be down before

anything happens." He spoke with the casual ignorance of someone who had never been around snow much.

At eleven they reached the peak of the trail. It was colder, the wind had picked up, and the clouds continued to grow more ominous. Kelly and Julie were getting nervous.

"How far do you think we have to go?" Kelly asked.

Brent consulted the map. "It looks like we're halfway, so I guess we have another five miles. But two of those miles are pretty much downhill. We should make good time."

"Should we keep going or stop for something to eat?" Julie's voice had a worried edge to it.

"I'd vote to keep going except that we need food to keep our energy up," Brent replied. "The temperature is dropping quite a bit. I say we stop just long enough to eat and then get going. I'm thinking about what Kelly's dad said about small, frequent meals being best."

The group nodded and dropped down behind a boulder that helped to cut off the wind. Reaching into his pack, Greg produced some bread, cheese, and an apple for each of them. In ten minutes they had polished off their small meal and were ready to push on.

Fifteen minutes later they came to a fork in the trail. Looking back at Brent, Greg, Kelly, and Julie waited for instructions. In the whipping wind he had a hard time reading the map. Finally, he looked up.

"Head to the right."

Greg surged forward, glad to finally have reached the downhill portion of their trip. The weather was beginning to scare him, too. Twenty minutes later they came out on a trail that carried the marker for the Appalachian Trail system. Confused, Greg stopped. Kelly's father hadn't told them about this. Brent skied up and looked at the sign silently. Down here, on level ground, the wind wasn't blowing so hard, and a close inspection of the map revealed his mistake at the fork.

"We have to go back up. I'm really sorry, you guys. It's my fault. I didn't read the map right up there a while ago."

Greg tried to be cheerful. "No problem, man. It's only twenty minutes back. We have plenty of time."

The twenty-minute trip turned into a forty-five minute struggle as they battled the terrain and the increasing wind. Kelly began to wish they had never come. Julie's face told her she was thinking the same thing. All of them were breathing hard when they broke out at the top and took the correct trail. For the next fifteen minutes they made good time.

Breaking out into a clearing, they gazed out over the mountain range that was all but obscured. Seconds later there was no evidence of them having been there—their tracks were covered. At four minutes past noon the storm hit the mountain with incredible fury. Instantly there were whiteout conditions. Huddled together the four could see each other, but the rest of the world was a white haze.

Kelly was scared. The trail was too near the edge of the mountain. What if they went over? She stood stock-still, afraid to move.

Brent took charge. By cupping his hand and yelling with all his might, he could just make himself heard over the storm and wind. "Head for the rock just down the path! That will block some of the wind! Stay close together!"

In the shelter of the rock, they didn't have to yell quite so loudly to be heard, but the world was still a white haze. Instinctively, Greg, Kelly, and Julie turned to Brent for direction. He had more experience in the outdoors than any of them. What were they supposed to do? Brent thought for several minutes before he spoke.

"We can't stay here," he said at last. "There isn't enough shelter, and we need to get down off the mountain. This storm looks like it could last for a while. We need to keep going. The trail is pretty wide. We should be able to follow it. I don't know what else to do."

"You're right that we can't stay here," Greg agreed. "We might be dressed for cross-country skiing, but we're not dressed for hanging out in a blizzard. We need to keep moving if we're going to stay warm."

Kelly and Julie just listened. They were content to let the boys take charge.

"Our greatest problem is going to be staying together," Brent continued. "If we get split up, we'll have real problems. In this snow you can hardly see three feet in front of you. I think we should tie ourselves together." Reaching into his pack, he pulled out the cord. "Tie this around your waist and then pass it back. Leave at least six feet in between. We're going to have to move really slow, but at least we'll be making progress."

Having joined themselves together with the cord, the four friends started down the trail. The rope made skiing even more difficult than the snow already had. Julie fell several times as she struggled to fight her growing cold and fear. Less than twenty minutes had passed before they all faced the inevitable truth. They were lost. Lost in what they would find out was the worst storm in ten years. Lost on a mountain they knew nothing about.

Brent's mind raced as he fought the numbing cold. He knew the others were looking to him. Their faces told him so. He had no answers except to keep moving. To stop would mean certain death. They would freeze to death without shelter. *Shelter.* Their goal would be to find shelter.

Shouting his decision to them, he was relieved to see their nods. Once more he turned and began to break a path. The snow was getting deeper and more difficult to ski through, but at least the effort was keeping him warm.

About thirty minutes had passed when Brent felt Julie fall again, only this time she didn't get up. He waited, but there was no movement at the end of the line. Turning around, he edged back toward her. She lay where she had fallen, tears frozen on her reddened cheeks. Greg and Kelly were leaning over her, but she was not responding. Slipping off his skis, Brent knelt down beside his girlfriend. "Julie." When he got no response, he yelled even louder, "Julie!" Slowly her eyes opened and focused on his face just inches from her own.

Shaking her head, she forced herself to speak. "Can't go . . . any further. Too cold . . . tired . . . need rest."

Brent shook his head. If she stayed where she was, she would freeze. She had to keep moving. Taking a deep breath, he reached down and shook her—hard. Her fluttering eyelids flew open as she gazed at him in fear. He didn't care. She had to move. Taking her arm, he hauled her to her feet. "You can't stay here. You *will* keep moving. You can't quit. I won't let you. Now *move!*"

With fresh tears flowing down her face, Julie continued to shuffle forward. Brent's will was keeping her going.

Kelly was fighting her own tears as the four trudged on. Were they going to die up here? Were they going to fight until they could fight no more, and then simply sit down to wait for death? She doubted Julie could go much further. Kelly prayed as she had never prayed before. And she continued to step slowly forward.

Julie fell two times more. Each time it took Brent's anger and force to keep her moving. One, then two hours passed as they pressed forward into the blinding whiteness. Kelly fell once, but Greg was right there to help her up and steady her. She allowed herself the luxury of leaning against him just for a moment, then she straightened and continued to move forward. Surely they would find shelter soon. It would be dark before too long.

Brent had all but given up when he made out the dim outline of a rock face through the snow. They were almost on it before he realized what they had stumbled upon. A cave! It wasn't much as caves went—not much more than a deep indention in the rock face—but the overhanging rock was cutting off the snow and provided some protection from the wind. Brent cheered silently as he glided to a halt. Julie, not looking where she was going, stumbled into him. He caught her before she fell again and gently led her into the opening. Kelly and Greg followed closely behind. Sinking down into the snow, Brent opened his pack and pulled out the plastic bags he found there.

He handed one to Julie and one to Kelly. "Here. Sit on these. They will offer some protection from the snow." Digging deeper, he pulled out two of the "space blankets." "Put these around you. We'll get a fire going as soon as we can. First, we need to block out more of the wind."

Brent realized they didn't have long before it was going to be dark. There was a lot to be done before then. Turning to Greg, he smiled at his friend. Greg responded with his own tired grin. At least they had shelter.

"We need to get branches and stuff to knock off the wind." Brent was still having to shout to be heard over the storm. "We can lean our skis up against the rock face and then lay the branches against them. It's not great, but it will help. We don't have much light left. Take this cord and tie yourself to this tree." He handed Greg the rope. "We can spread out from here. We don't need to get lost after all this."

Greg nodded, and they set to work. Moving in opposite directions, they ranged to the end of their ropes, breaking off branches from the surrounding firs and spruces. The full boughs would offer much protection. Carrying large armfuls, they stumbled back to the cave. Several trips provided enough to satisfy Brent.

"Now we need firewood. We'll get as much as we can and pile it inside the cave."

The two boys were ready to fall over from exhaustion when Brent decided that the pile in the cave was adequate. When they finally stumbled in from the cold, they saw that Kelly had broken twigs and limbs and laid an excellent fire. Their starter sticks should take care of the wetness of the wood.

Brent allowed them a small rest and then continued to drive forward. "We need to take care of shelter. It's almost dark. Greg, untie your rope from the tree. We're going to need it to lash the branches on."

Thirty minutes later their shelter was complete. It did indeed make a tremendous difference. The lean-to effect the branches created was stopping the wind and snow and would do a passable job of holding in any available warmth. They had left a small opening at one end that they could crawl through, and Brent had cut a small hole at the top to allow the smoke from the fire to escape. Grabbing the last armfuls of boughs, the boys moved inside. They took the branches and made a thick covering on the ground inside the cave. Once the entire area was generously covered, Brent cut the plastic bags open and laid them over the greenery. It wasn't great, but it would give them a dry place to sit and lay.

Kelly continued to sit with Julie who was shaking from the cold. Her friend seemed to have lost all will to fight. She just looked around dully at all the activity. Kelly had added her space blanket to Julie's in hopes that she would get warm.

Brent dug into the pack again and pulled out the fire starters and matches. It was touch and go for a while, but finally the wet wood caught and began to burn brightly. Within twenty minutes their little shelter began to warm. Kelly felt her spirits rise with the temperature. She convinced Julie to move closer to the flames. Gradually, Kelly saw the life return to her friend's eyes.

Brent leaned over and spoke softly to Greg. "Fix all of us something to eat, will you? There's something else I want to do outside." With those words he disappeared into the storm once more.

Greg and Kelly pulled out all the food and inspected their supply: eight thick slices of bread, about a pound of cheese, four apples, two oranges, sandwich meat, and a handful of cookies.

"I sure am glad you guys packed all this food this morning. I laughed at you then, but God knew we would need it. We can make this last for a while."

"Me, too!" Greg's response was fervent. He reached into Kelly's and Julie's packs and pulled out their water bottles. "Brent has a large tin cup in his pack," he whispered to Kelly. "Let's heat up some water for Julie. It will probably help her feel better."

"Good idea." Kelly looked around their shelter until she found a large, flat rock. Sitting it close to the fire, she poured water into the cup and placed it on the rock.

When Brent stumbled back in thirty minutes later, Kelly was lifting a cup of the hot liquid to Julie's lips. She looked in alarm at her exhausted friend. "What have you been doing, Brent? You look beat!"

He shook his head silently and dropped down on the ground next to the fire. After several minutes he spoke. "There was too much wind coming in through the branches. I went out and packed a thick layer of snow all the way to the top of the shelter. It will do a better job of keeping this place warm. Funny. It's the snow that's causing the problem, but it's also going to help us. I sure am glad I spent so much time talking to your dad. He's the one who told me all this stuff."

Greg slapped him on the shoulder. "You've been awesome, man. I can already feel the place getting warmer. And there are no drafts. It could actually get cozy in here."

"My dad." Kelly's voice was troubled. "Our folks are going to be frantic. They'll have no way of knowing if we're okay, and I don't imagine anyone can come up the mountain to look for us in this storm."

"They won't send out a rescue team until the snow lets up and the sun rises tomorrow," Brent agreed. "At least they knew where we were going. I have no idea where we are on this mountain, but we're going to make it. We have a warm shelter and plenty of instant water waiting for us outside. Our food may run out, but we'll be out of here before that becomes a problem."

Food and hot water revived them all. Julie even sat up and began to take an interest in what was happening. Suddenly Kelly looked up.

"It's New Year's Eve!"

"Huh?" All three friends spoke simultaneously.

"It's New Year's Eve. We need to celebrate. I think we should have our own New Year's Eve service. We may be stuck on a mountain in a blizzard, but we're still about to start another year."

SEVENTEEN

Greg looked at Brent and Julie, smiled, and shrugged his shoulders. "She's right, you know. We may not be in the place of our choice, but in just a few hours we're going to see another new year come in on top of this mountain. We really do have a lot to celebrate."

"You're right about that!" Julie replied fervently. "We could be frozen stiff somewhere, but instead we're almost warm in this little cave. I'm just glad to be alive."

Looking at Kelly, Greg asked, "So what do we do for our celebration? It's your idea, so you just got put in charge."

Kelly thought for a few minutes and then smiled. "We definitely need to sing. Singing always makes me feel better." As the others nodded agreement, she led off in one of her favorite songs. For the next hour they defied the snow and cold as they launched from one tune to the next. They ran the gamut of everything they knew—secular and Christian, pop, country, and gospel.

When their voices finally fell silent, Kelly looked around at her three friends and gave them all a warm smile. "You know, I'm kind of liking it here. I believe this would qualify as what my dad fondly calls a 'bonding experience.' Whenever we go through hard times as a family, he says we can either let it destroy us or use it to draw us closer together. I feel so close to you guys right now."

Greg, Julie, and Brent nodded their heads in solemn affirmation.

"I also feel really close to God," Kelly continued. "When we were out on the mountain in the snow today, I wanted to give up so bad. I didn't want to keep going. I wanted to lay down in the snow and pretend it wasn't happening. I just kept praying and somehow God kept me going. I think the neatest thing, though, was that I could actually feel him with me. When it got the hardest, it was almost as if he were there, coaching me on, telling me I could make it. So I just kept sliding one ski in front of the other. The longer I'm a Christian, the more real Jesus seems to me. I think when we get down off this mountain, I'm going to see this whole experience as a very positive thing."

Brent reached over for several pieces of wood and added them to the fire. His three friends could sense he wanted to talk, so they sat and waited. Several minutes passed as they stared into the flames. "I have to thank y'all for being the best friends anyone could ever have," he finally said. "When we were out on the mountain today, I was really surprised to find myself fighting so hard to stay alive. It was strange to realize I was fighting for myself just as hard as I was fighting for y'all. I knew y'all were depending on me, but I also knew that I wanted to live."

Pausing, he stared deeply into the fire. "I told Greg the other night that part of me wanted to live and part of me wanted to die. I realize now that *all* of me wants to live. I know God saved our lives out there. I didn't find this cave. He led us to it. I have to believe God has a purpose for all our lives—mine included. When I thought about how hard I fought this storm, I really saw that all of us have huge storms in our life. We can either choose to fight them with God's help or just lay down and let them destroy us. I almost chose to quit fighting. I still am amazed that I'm getting another chance. I don't want to mess this one up. I know now that I have God and I have close friends who will hang in there with me through problems. I intend to make it."

Greg cheered silently as he gave his friend a big grin. "That's the way to talk, man! If you've gotten all that through your thick head, then this storm is worth it. I'm with Kelly. I think I'm starting to enjoy this."

"I've had a really hard time understanding how Brent could try to kill himself," Julie said quietly, after a few moments of silence. "But I think I understand more now. Today, on the mountain, I wanted to give up so bad. I was so cold and so afraid. I just wanted to lay down and let everything go away. If Brent hadn't kept me going, I'm sure I would have died. I just didn't have the will to keep going." Looking at Brent, she spoke softly, "You saved my life. Thanks."

Brent just shrugged and smiled. "I'd say you're worth it, Julie."

"I'm glad you think so. I need to say more, though. I hope it doesn't make you angry." Taking a deep breath, she struggled for the right words. "When you tried to kill yourself, it really tore me up inside. I felt sure it was somehow my fault. If I had done the right thing or said the right thing, maybe you wouldn't have done it. I felt so guilty and so much like a failure. I hated myself. Kelly kept telling me it wasn't my fault. Once I began to accept that, then I started to get angry."

She took a deep breath and stared down at the ground. "Killing yourself would have hurt so many people. Especially me. You would have ended *your* problems, but they would have just started for the rest of us. We would have had to live with all the memories and the guilt. I think until this afternoon I was still angry with you. Now I think I'm just hurt. I understand more, but I'm still hurt. I know I shouldn't take it personally. It's not like you were trying to hurt *me*. But sometimes the heart doesn't go along with what the head is saying." Grinding to a halt, she continued to stare at the ground. It was obvious she was afraid of Brent's reaction.

He did the best thing possible. Brent stood and walked over to where Julie sat hunched on the ground and wrapped his arms around her. Julie's tears began to flow. Brent rocked her gently until her sobbing ceased. Only then did he speak, "I don't blame you for feeling the way you do. It wasn't until I thought you were giving up that I realized how much pain I would have left behind if I had killed myself. I was mad at you today because I thought you should be willing to fight to stay alive for *us*. When I got angry, I realized how stupid it was. And then I saw what killing myself would have done to everyone. Funny, though, you don't think about other people's pain when you're hurting that bad yourself. I will now, though." Hugging Julie warmly, he continued, "Thanks for being honest. I needed to know how you're feeling. I hope we can start over and go from here."

Julie looked up. Her tremulous smile was all the answer he needed.

Greg gave a huge sigh of satisfaction. "I think this is the best New Year's Eve I've ever spent. I know that I've learned a big lesson today about how precious life is. When I was out on that mountain, not sure if we were going to make it, I was thinking about all that I wanted to do with my life. When you think it's about to be over, it's amazing how many things you wished you'd done. You wish you'd said certain things to people, not said certain things to people. I realized that you never know how much longer you have to live, so you need to make the most of every day. My father calls it 'sucking all you can from life.' I want to do that from now on. I hope I never take life for granted again." Greg looked around. "I can't think of a better way to start the New Year than for us to spend some time praying. What do you think?"

Nodding heads resulted in a long prayer time as they prayed for each other, their parents, and the people who would be looking for them. Peace covered their little shelter like a blanket. Standing as a group, they wrapped their arms around each other in a big hug and stood that way for several minutes.

Finally Brent stepped back. "We've got some things that need to be taken care of. The fire is dying down. Kelly, do you mind adding more wood? Greg, I think we need to melt some more snow for water. And we should get some sleep so we'll have the strength to ski out in the morning if the storm stops. One of us needs to keep the fire going, though. How about if you and I take turns?"

Greg nodded. "No problem."

"Nothing doing, Brent." Julie said firmly. "We're in this together. We *all* should take turns."

Brent grinned. "Whatever you say. If you want to stay up and stoke the fire, I won't complain about the extra sleep I'll get!"

The storm raged on with unabated fury while Brent, Julie, and Kelly drifted off to sleep peacefully under their space blankets. Greg manned the first watch over the fire.

• • •

"How's it look out there?"

Greg rolled over and spoke to Brent who had just crawled back in from his early-morning inspection of the storm. Throughout the long night, the four of them had switched stations at the fire. Brent had pulled the last leg.

"Not too good. The wind isn't blowing quite so hard, but the snow is still thick. It looks like we've gotten a foot since yesterday."

Kelly and Julie woke up and stretched. "Good morning," they said in unison.

Greg and Brent echoed back their greeting, but quickly returned to their conversation.

"What do you think we should do?" Greg asked. "Do you think we could make it out of here?"

Brent shook his head. "I don't think it's a good idea to try. We still have no idea where we are, and the visibility isn't much better than yesterday. We could get lost pretty fast and be back to hunting for shelter. I think we need to stay put. The storm has to end sometime. We'll have a better chance of finding our way off the mountain then."

"I think Brent is right," Kelly joined in the conversation. "At least we're safe here. I bet we could even build a second fire if we can get enough wood. We could make this place absolutely toasty. I have no desire to be floundering around on this mountain again."

Everyone in agreement, the four made plans for their day. They decided it would be best to assume they would be stranded for a while and to prepare accordingly. Before they began work, they rationed the food and passed portions out for breakfast. A slice of bread with one piece of sandwich meat didn't fill their empty stomachs, but it was something. At least they had plenty to drink. Lots of water would take the edge off their hunger, Brent insisted.

Once they had eaten, they set to work. Brent and Greg decided to reinforce their shelter to better hold in the warmth. Tying themselves once more to the tree, they spread out in different directions and brought back huge armfuls of boughs. They laid them against the snow Brent had packed the night before and then added another thick layer of snow. Their lean-to wall was now almost eight inches thick. Greg was thankful for the sturdiness of the skis holding it in position.

While the boys worked, Kelly and Julie used their ropes and scrounged for wood. It was hard going. The deep snow made it necessary to dig down into the drifts and search for sticks and thick limbs small enough to take inside. Back and forth they went, hauling all their arms could carry. It was almost noon before Brent and Greg joined them. One more hour of work and they had a huge pile of wood stacked in their emergency shelter.

"I think you can have your second fire now, Kelly. I made another small opening at the other end of the lean-to. With a fire at both ends we really should be quite warm. We might even start to get hot!" Brent said with a look of deep satisfaction.

Greg built a second fire while Kelly gave each person a slice of cheese and an apple for lunch. They could all have a small supper, and then they would be out of food. Large quantities of water would have to suffice. Once they had all eaten, they laid down to sleep and restore the energy they had expended that morning. Julie volunteered to tend the fire while the others slept.

When Kelly awoke from her nap, she silently slipped over to where Julie sat. Whispering, she leaned close to her friend. "Let's let the boys sleep as long as they can. They have to be exhausted. We can keep things going for a while. Do you want to get some sleep?"

"Maybe in a little bit. Right now I'm just enjoying feeling warm. The two fires have turned this place into a castle." Julie whispered her words as well and then lapsed into silence.

The two girls sat in companionable silence for an hour while the boys slept peacefully. Finally Julie crawled under her space blanket and slept. Brent was just beginning to wake up when Kelly tilted her head to listen.

"What is it, Kelly? Do you hear something?" Brent's voice was sharp.

"No. Isn't that wonderful?"

"Huh?" Brent's voice was groggy with sleep.

"The storm. I think it's stopped! I can't hear the wind anymore. It's quiet outside."

Greg was just waking up and heard her words. Cocking his head, his face split into a wide grin. "I think you're right, Kelly. I'm going to take a look." Pulling on his coat, he slipped out the opening. His voice floated back in seconds later. "Hey! You guys got to come out here. Wait till you see this!"

His excited voice prompted all of them to scramble out the lean-to opening. They stood in awe of what was before them. The storm had definitely stopped. Through a clearing in the trees they could see the last rays of the sunlight as the golden orb slipped below the horizon of jagged peaks. Its final act had been to spread fingers of rose, purple, and orange in a kaleidoscope of colors across the sky. As they watched, the colors deepened in a final glorious farewell before they began to be absorbed by the darkness of the approaching night.

"Hello!" A call wafted up the ridge.

Kelly jerked her head in its direction. "What was that?"

Brent was already scrambling back into the lean-to. "It's a person—probably part of the rescue team. Y'all start yelling. I'll get the whistle."

For the next five minutes yells and whistles erupted from their camp. Finally they saw two people appear below them in the woods. The two waved their arms to indicate they had spotted them and then picked their way up the slope. They were within yards of the camp before the four friends could make out the outfits of the Appalachian Ski Patrol and see the wide grins the two men were wearing.

"Boy, are we glad to see you! I'm Mike. This is Nathan." They shook hands with each of them. "You guys okay?"

"We're fine." Brent replied. "But we sure are glad to see you guys. We're almost out of food."

"We figured that. We've got plenty. We've been searching since early morning. We were getting ready to give up and head back. It will be dark soon. What happened?"

Brent and Greg filled them in quickly on the details. When Mike and Nathan crawled into their lean-to, they were obviously impressed. "This is quite a place," Mike remarked. "Where did you learn how to do this?"

"It was all Brent's doing. We just followed orders." Kelly was quick to give him the credit.

Brent shrugged. "Kelly's father told me how to do it. I never had any idea it would come in so handy so quick."

Mike and Nathan were unpacking food as they talked. In minutes, they had given the four friends large packs of trailmix, huge hunks of cheese with crackers, and an abundance of fruit. They even demolished a large container of pasta salad. Within minutes their energy returned. While they ate, Mike radioed down to the central unit.

"We've got them. They're in good condition. They've actually made themselves quite a little retreat up here," Mike chuckled. "They were hungry, but we've taken care of that. They're fine to bring down off the mountain tonight. Send the snowmobiles up." He gave the dispatcher directions to their location.

Greg, Brent, Julie, and Kelly exchanged delighted looks. Snowmobiles! Now *that* was the way to travel.

Mike turned back to them. "We have about thirty minutes before they get here. Where are your skis and stuff? Let's get all your gear together so we can load quickly." He looked puzzled when Brent nodded toward the wall of the lean-to. Then he looked more closely. "Smart! Pretty smart. You used the skis as the support for your lean-to," he observed. "That's what I call using your head as well as all available materials." He laughed again. "Nathan, I think we need to add these guys to our ski patrol."

"Brent gets all the credit," Greg spoke up for his friend. "He's the one who knew what to do. We just did what he told us. He was awesome! Without him I don't think we would have made it."

Brent blushed but sent a grateful look to Greg. "It was no big deal," he protested.

It took them the thirty minutes to dismantle their shelter and collect all their gear. By the time they were done, the sky had turned into a starry canopy that gave no hint of the fury that had raged for a day and a half. They heard the roar of the snowmobiles in the distance. It was another ten minutes before sweeping lights illuminated their position and six snowmobiles zoomed up. After excited greetings, the six on foot each climbed on behind a member of the ski patrol. Skis and gear were lashed on carefully, and they were off.

Kelly thrilled to the adventure as they zoomed down the trails. Thankful for the warmth of the thick snowsuits the ski patrol had given each of them, she snuggled down and enjoyed the ride. She also felt her heart swell at the thought of reunion with her parents. She knew how worried they must have been. She had also been reminded how precious they were to her. She could hardly wait to see them and Emily.

The others were sharing similar thoughts. Even Brent. In spite of the problems in his family, he knew he loved both of his parents.

In an hour they were let off at the bottom of the mountain and swept into their families' arms. Julie's parents had come up as soon as they got the news. Brent's mother and father were there as well. No one was ashamed of the tears that flowed. Questions flew back and forth as chaos broke loose.

Finally Scott Marshall took control. Stepping back, he raised his voice and commanded everyone's attention. "Let's go back to the cabin. We can get the whole story there. I'm sure these four would like a hot shower and some hot food." Turning to the ski patrol, he once more expressed his appreciation. "You guys have been wonderful. I don't know what we would have done without you. Thank you!"

"You're welcome, Mr. Marshall. That's what we're here for. I wish all the stories had happy endings like yours. Take these four kids home. They need some rest! You can drop off the snowsuits at the ski center on your way out tomorrow." The head of the ski patrol waved his hand and hopped into his truck.

In minutes the entire group was surging into the cabin.

EIGHTEEN

Greg woke early the next morning. Rolling over he saw that Brent was already out of bed and gone. Glancing at his watch, he noticed it was only six-thirty, but his long nap the afternoon before in the lean-to had rested him too much to sleep late this morning.

Last night had been wonderful. The reunion between the families had lasted until almost midnight when his father had finally called a halt to it. Exhausted, the four friends had taken hot showers and fallen into bed.

Greg flung the covers back, slipped on his sweats, and went in search of Brent. He had been talking to his parents on the porch last night for quite a while. Greg was curious to find out how it went. He found Brent on the front porch, leaning over to watch the morning sky begin to lighten with the approaching day.

Brent looked up as Greg slipped through the door and walked over to join him. "Good morning," he said. "You're up early."

Greg leaned against the railing next to him. "I could say the same for you."

"Yeah. I had a lot to think about. I wanted some quiet. Once everybody gets up, it's going to be a zoo."

"You got that right. Do you want to talk about it?"

"I guess so." Brent turned to face Greg. "I had a long talk with my parents last night."

"Yeah. I saw you talking to them."

"My being lost on the mountain got them really talking since all this mess started. They realized and admitted that they have put me in the middle, trying to hurt each other. They know they *have* hurt each other, but they said they never meant to hurt me. Both of them apologized and asked me to forgive them." He paused in thought.

"So did you?" Greg questioned.

"Of course. I've done a lot of stupid things lately, not thinking about who I would hurt in the process. It seemed kind of hypocritical not to forgive them for their stupid mistakes." He paused again. "Seems funny, saying that your parents do stupid things, but I think I'm beginning to see that they're human, too. Just because they're older doesn't mean they aren't going to make mistakes."

Greg nodded.

"Anyway," Brent continued, "I think I've hoped for a long time that my parents would get back together. I'm sure that's part of the reason I resented Allison so much. She was keeping that from happening—at least that's what I thought. I finally understood last night that their marriage is over. Neither one of them has any desire to see it work.

Dad is going to marry Allison next month. I can either keep hoping, or I can just make the best of it." He sighed. "There are always going to be times when life hands you tough situations. It's how you deal with them that counts."

Brent leaned out over the railing and was quiet for several minutes. Greg waited, sensing he wasn't through.

"I chose death as a way to handle it once," Brent finally said. "From now on I'm going to choose life—life walking hand in hand with God."

About the Author

Ginny Williams grew up loving and working with horses. When she got older, she added a love for teenagers to the top of her list. She admits she goes through withdrawal when she doesn't have kids around her, not that that has happened much in her fifteen years of youth ministry.

Ginny lives on a large farm outside of Richmond, Virginia, with her husband, Louis, two Labrador retrievers, a large flock of Canada geese, and a herd of deer. When she's not writing or speaking to youth groups, she can be found using her degree in recreation. She loves to travel and play. She bikes, plays tennis, windsurfs, rides horses (of course!), plays softball—she'll do anything that's fun! She's planning a bike trip across the country, and she's waiting for her chance to skydive and bungee jump.

**Capturing the Spirit
of the Next Generation...**

The Class of 2000
by Ginny Williams

Second Chances

At 15 years old, Kelly finds her life in sudden turmoil when her widowed father decides to remarry. Struggling with bitter feelings, Kelly determines that she'll never accept her father's wife. But a beautiful black horse, a special friend, and a daring rescue from a burning barn give Kelly a different perspective on those she loves...and a chance to start over with her new stepmother.

A Matter of Trust

God changed Kelly's heart, but now she's finding it difficult sometimes for her actions to follow. Conflict at home threatens to tear the family apart. But when her beloved horse almost dies, Kelly discovers strength and support from an unlikely source—her stepmom.

Lost-and-Found Friend

Kelly's friend Brent is a very sensitive, very intense person who is adept at hiding his troubles. When pressures at home become overwhelming, Brent attempts suicide. Concerned friends, a ski trip, and a life-threatening snowstorm help Brent realize there are alternative ways to solve his problems.